MW00611358

"Now we have a down-to-earth Edward Dunkel, whose vast and expertise to his analysis of the manag...... needed by all artists if they are to successfully confront the stresses, individualized fears, and tensions that are the reality of the music business. *THE AUDITION PROCESS* is really a working manual, a probing treatment of approaches in developing successful outlooks and modes of confidence in gaining strength that lends power to performances. The organizational structure of the book lends itself to systematic exploration of the principal problem areas arising before and during an audition with helpful guidelines in development of coping strategies and techniques to deal with diverse stress situations. He offers a veritable stockpile of workable techniques that have been found to be effective in the creative arts. Dunkel has made a significant contribution in an area that has need of greater insights."

Opera Guide, April 1990

■

"...contains much excellent advice not only for musicians, but for people in any walk of life."

Canadian Federation of Music Teachers Association, Spring 1990

■

"Stuart Dunkel's book is full of practical and helpful information for dealing with the anxiety and stress often associated with audition and performance situations in the professional music world. He approaches the subject from the perspective of someone who has "been there" and has been able to triumph over his fears and anxieties. He give good, helpful advice to help musicians conquer their fears and manage stress. This is an important book for the serious performer, professional or amateur."

Dr. Robert Sirota - Dean of Boston University School of Music

■

"Stuart Dunkel is eloquent about the anxiety of the musical audition...Professor Dunkel's book is intended not for musicians alone, but for anyone who is occasionally in the public eye."

The Link, Boston University Nov. 1990

"There are many apt observations and useful advice that might well help auditioners brace for the test, and live happily ever after."
The Juilliard Journal, May 1990

■

"It is a highly readable manual of 'practical' suggestions for the person who has committed to a career or near-career in musical performance. I find especially good the concept that a person's self-worth really should not be related to success or failure in one area."
Professor Rudolf E. Radocy, Editor *JRME*

■

"...a very truthful and useful book...the author speaks with a first-hand voice that one must be willing to accept the realities and responsibilities of life as a musician. He further discusses the importance of maintaining one's professional integrity. This book deserves to be included in the essential reading list of every serious musician not only for successful auditions but also for successful living. This book would be appropriate as a textbook for a music pedagogy course."
Council for Research in Music Education Bulletin, Sang-Hie Lee, University of Alabama

■

"The focus is on the individual and his growth as a person in regard to the audition procedure. Dunkel has captured the essence of many coping strategies and categorized them in relation to specific areas for physical stress and mental anxiety.

"The audition is part of the process of the music business and is not an end in itself. Performers, or would-be performers, tend to professionally live or die after one audition. Dunkel's consistent effort is to have the reader understand that auditioning can be a positive experience. Through the many useful strategies given, the reader should be better prepared prior to, during, and after the audition."
Steven Hauser, *American Music Teacher*, May, 1991

THE AUDITION PROCESS
ANXIETY MANAGEMENT AND COPING STRATEGIES

Stuart Edward Dunkel

THE AUDITION PROCESS
ANXIETY MANAGEMENT
AND COPING STRATEGIES

by

Stuart Edward Dunkel

JUILLIARD PERFORMANCE GUIDES No. 3

PENDRAGON PRESS
STUYVESANT, NY

The Juilliard Performance Guides
    1. *Toward an Authentic Interpretation of the Organ Works of César Franck* by Rollin Smith ISBN 0-918728-25-8 (1983)
    2. *The Fables of La Fontaine: Vocal settings and interpretations* by John Metz ISBN 0-918728-26-6 (1985)

Cover painting: *Church Scene* by Stuart Edward Dunkel

Library of Congress Cataloging-in-Publication Data
Dunkel, Stuart Edward.
    The audition process : anxiety management and coping strategies / by Stuart Edward Dunkel.
      p. cm. -- (Juilliard performance guides: no 3)
    Includes bibliographical refences.
    ISBN 0-945193-02-5
    ISBN 0-945193-35-1
    1. Music--Performance--Auditions--Psychological aspects. 2. Stage fright. I. Title. II. Series.
ML3830.D9 1990
7891.4'3--dc20   89-37075   CIP MN

꧁꧂

CONTENTS

PREFACE

When I began my doctoral studies, I had taken some 36 orchestral auditions. In trying to secure a position as an oboist in a symphony orchestra, I found that there was more to the ritual of auditioning than merely performing well; there was also a psychological factor that had to be understood. Approaching an audition with a healthy frame of mind not only made the audition pleasant, but I also found that a healthy mind-set helped reduce the power and terror inherent in the trauma of setting myself up for failure and rejection. As I took more auditions, I noticed that my ups and downs, my frustrations, and my depressions were subject to how I perceived the end result of winning or losing. By studying the anxiety management techniques of various psychologists and schools of psychotherapy, I was able to apply some principles to help me with my particular problems. I became more curious to explore the many ideas that other disciplines, such as eastern philosophy and sports psyching, offered to increase optimum performance.

There have been writings specifically for the purpose of reducing performance anxiety in fields other than music, such as acting and psychology. The school of cognitive therapy offers much along these lines. A few books are available for musicians that are geared towards better performance. In my opinion, these books offer a few excellent suggestions but do not present enough insights to cover the gamut of frustations I feel.

One exciting result of the research I have been doing is that many people have consulted with me as to their particular fears in taking auditions. I have thus been able to refer them to some principles that have given them insight and consolation.

I want to thank Dr. Barry Brook for helping me arrive at this topic and his guidance in organizing my thoughts. Thanks go to my brother, Dr. Allan Dunkel, a wonderful psychologist in his own right, whose insights into academia and psychology have steered me in the right direction. I appreciate the patience of my wife, Kristen Severson, who helped me with editing and moral support. I thank the musicians and psychologists I have consulted: Michael Colgrass,

Michele Parker, Dr. Perry Belfer, Daniel Silver, Dr. Robert Kurlantzick, Mikki Schiff, Kristen Severson, Connie Beckley, Jacqualine Carlton, Dr. Lawrence Dunkel, Dr. David Whitten, Suellen Hershman, Elma Kanefield, Robert Bennett, Janice Bennett, Alice Shields, Elaine Douvas, Ralph Gomberg, Peter Bowman, and Dr. Ernest Lozano.

PREFACE TO THE 2ND EDITION

In the year since this book was published I have given seminars and lectures about performing. I received many new insights and have learned a great deal from this interaction "in the field", and welcome the opportunity presented by this second preface to offer a few comments from my present vantage point.

Auditioning and performing consume all of our energies when we are dedicated to our craft, yet we must find a balance between the total involvement in our work and the wonderful selfish enjoyment of our life outside of that work. Having a perspective on what is meaningful in our lives clearly helps us choose how to make our life enjoyable. A career in the arts can have many ups and downs; moments of elation and intense bliss followed suddenly by depression and futile hopelessness. The intensity that we have poured into our work will mirror the desperation we feel at auditions. This book is about pain—physical, emotional and psychological. It is about my personal experiences fighting the dark side of a beautiful profession. Taking an audition or having a stressful performance makes us look into the abyss of our own personal fears; fears as diverse and intense as we make them, ranging from the mundane to the existential. Indeed, performance is a microcosm of life condensed into a few minutes.

In the hope of finding a secure orchestral position I have taken many auditions. I won the first professional audition I took. However, my teacher advised me that I should not go to Sao Paulo, Brazil as I was only a sophomore at Boston University. I also won the second audition: the English Horn position of the Springfield (Massachusetts) Symphony. I played a season there, and when my friends were getting their contracts for the next year and I had not received mine, I called to inquire about it. They said, "Oh, didn't we tell you? It was only a one year position." I became a veteran at that moment. My audition profile has more curves to it than Eugene Ormandy's beat. I have been a finalist for the principal oboe post at the Metropolitan Opera, the orchestras of Grand Rapids, Fort Wayne,

New Haven, New Orleans, Hong Kong, Florida,Toluca (Mexico), and a semi-finalist in Cleveland, Washington, Boston, the Met once again, and at an orchestra in Germany. There were dozens of other times however when the Fates were not with me and my confidence was shaken. These ups and downs are an integral part of performing, for they activate our insecurities and self doubts.

These insecurities which arise in tense situations need to be immediately addressed, or we are doomed to repeat them. Problems of doubting one's abilities, one's control over situations, and one's self-image must be answered with a rational self-statement or comeback followed by emotional relaxation. Emotional relaxation is simply achieved by reminding ourselves that everything is fine the way it is; that we are wanted and needed for the task at hand. In the belief that our actions are fulfilling the need of either the committee or orchestra, performing becomes a labor of love instead of a survival test.

Performing carries an implied obligation that we must execute the music perfectly. Indeed, we strive toward that goal; yet in order to feel free to be perfect, we must give ourselves the freedom to make mistakes. I tell myself that as long as I intend to do the best job I can, whatever happens is fine, for I can control my intent but I cannot control the elusive moment of that picture-perfect future. If I am not at my peak today, it does not destroy my world. At the moment of performance I must trust the hand of destiny and my natural abilities and let the cards fall where they may. I do my best and accept what happens. This frees me to perform without a feeling of being bound up by rules and procedures. I can then view the performance as a time to show off my skills and insights and to flaunt the beauty I create. In that moment of creation I try to amuse myself, not others, and that in turn make my performance meaningful to others. It makes me feel worthy to be on stage.

There's a character within me whom I call Dennis the Menace, who likes to cause trouble and excitement. He siezes the slightest opportunity to take all sorts of risks, and creates such wondrous things that I just sit back and let him go where he will. He is very creative and finds variations inside variations. I let him out to play when I feel the greatest need to go beyond my limits. Of course, I suppress him when it is not appropriate or my feet would never touch the ground. If I let him run amok inside my head all the time, I could not be responsible to even get to the concerts on time. He is a valuable tool in my professional life although no one sees him.

One of the major pitfalls to performing is the fear of making a mistake. I have suffered with such intense worry over this that it forced me to find an attitude that allowed me to function. I have performed with three of the top 5 symphony orchestras in this country. I was amazed at how the first rehearsals were littered with bad rhythm, terrible intonation, and chaotic style. I was doubly astonished at the second rehearsal for the rhythm was solid, the intonation corrected, and the style unified. These professional musicians know that a rehearsal serves to present yourself and your interpretation to your colleagues and conductor and then work with it to make music into magic. To view your performance as a rehearsal or practice, where you risk putting your best into it, and not an examination, where you try *not* to do something, it is possible to put yourself at ease to be open to all that is around you. When you are scared and defensive you are in closed focus, aware only of your inner world and oblivious to the support and wonder about you. I have given up the notion of a flawless concert for that reason; I would rather go out there and try to push my creative technique to make the magic happen (and sometimes a string broken, a wild note, water in a key, or a snapped mallot will result from it).

If I notice a mistake while performing, I'm not flustered. I realize that if I take the time to notice it, my mind is in the past and I lose the concentration of the present passage. During a performance it is not productive to be analytical and in a thinking mode. I try to rid my mind of any unfocused chatter and instead, fill it with one idea, usually a musical gesture I want to execute. I remember the fact that the mind can only think of one thing at a time and I tell myself what to do. When I notice a mistake, I accept it and quickly proceed to the present moment. Accepting the mistake means I have noted it and should it come up again I can be prepared to handle it differently.

We all have fears of certain things going awry in a performance. For some it is the fear of running out of air when they play, a shaky bow, lack of concentration, fear that everyone is better than they are, panic after a mistake; for others there is fear of physical tension ruining a passage or of always making a mistake at the same place. In order to have a career, one has to conquer the persistent fears in order to function.

"You can't get it right until you get it wrong" is a saying among painters. In order to achieve success you have to fail first. On canvas the oil paint takes time to dry so you can change it when its still wet. In music you have one chance to recreate what is in your musical imagination. In your head, then, you have to have a clearly worked out model before it is actualized. You then have rehearsed correctly at least once and all you have to do is execute it.

When I am nervous I talk to myself with the voice of my trusted teacher. He says "Do your best and accept what happens. trust in yourself, accept yourself and your faults". If I find such self-talk bothersome I don't do it, I keep my outward attention on the music and the situation. I try to understand that intent is more important than the actual product. This relieves much of my worry about mistakes. Oftentimes I find my concentration disrupted by the need for approval from my friends, conductors, or the audience. At those times helpful self-talk brings me back into reality.

Worry is my greatest enemy. It creates fear and doubt, and is what turns the physical audition into a psychological one as well. Sometimes it is hard enough just getting there, let alone performing with a good attitude. In the past, my worry escalated into a downward phobic spiral that made it difficult to get on stage for a period of two years. My search for help with my problems resulted in the contents of this book. Everyone has to come to terms with worry over self-image, with doubting our control over a situation, and with questioning our ability to do the job.

During one such self-analysis, I realized that worry is my creative mind imaging the worst future. I now try to use my mind-power to imagine a future of success and in so doing I already know how it feels to win. Having experienced it once, I can rest assured that it will no doubt happen again in what seems to be the combat zone.

Often I find myself repeating my two most important words: hope and resilience. This mantra helps me out of the downward spiral which develops when things don't go as I would like. Hope describes the feeling that things will be fine in the future, and is at the time of doubt and frustration that I rely on it. Its a magical feeling which when accepted, allows me to access spirits higher than myself and even reach that deep unconscious part of me that is deserving of respect. It frees the weighty burden of being perfect and allows me the freedom to be me.

I think all artists know what resilience is. It picks us up when we falter. I'm not sure when it is that I say to myself, "that's enough moping, pick yourself up," but doing so creates a new start to a failed past. It is very important to be able to excuse what has just happened and to start again with a rejuvenated spirit. Resilience is a magical concept also.

Sometimes the sensitivity required to make us good artists, makes us too insecure to function up to our capabilities. I try to use various emotions to my benefit. One has to understand the hierarchy of power each emotion holds and then know how to recall certain ones for certain moments.

Guilt and fear are emotions which are usually turned inward and which are destructive to performance. They bring such intense negative energy that we sometimes cannot perform because of them. They bring confusion and doubt and paralyzing thoughts of failure. When I have such feelings I try to cut through the negativity by bringing a stronger emotion to the front, thereby ridding myself of self-destructive images. Anger is the key. Being able to bring up intense pictures of rage, in whatever fearful circumstance, can dispel all those feelings of fear (and guilt). We can conquer much if we are able to access our positive emotional undercurrents.

When I am on stage and feeling particularly nervous or out of control I know that I have to make a sudden shift in emotion or I will be trapped in an unenjoyable experience. To help me feel enraged I bring up images of childhood scuffs, abusive teachers and uncomfortable exchanges with colleagues and conductors. I put up my make-believe movie screen and imagine a loud, vivid, and colorful scene of an encounter and run it though again and again to bring up that wanted anger. I use that angry emotion directed to specific people or events to fill me with an intense energy. This red heat gives me the tool to overpower the feeling of fear I sometimes have when performing. Feeling angry brings me to a place where I feel I have control, and that I have the right to be onstage. Once in control I can then bring a stronger emotion to quench the anger: love. Love is a feeling that is more powerful than either anger or fear, because it allows us to reward ourselves for a good effort.

Its amazing how the inner body has its own language. Physical problems and distracting feelings can be universally heard in expressions like: jumping out of ones skin, be on pins and needles, have one's heart in one's mouth, make ones hair stand on end, makes one's blood run cold, makes one's teeth chatter, takes one's breath away, scare the life out of, scare the pants off of, makes one flesh creep, perfectionism leads to paralysis, and being scared stiff. The fear of experiencing unpleasant physical sensations while performing can become a mild phobia for those overly concerned with it. I like to create my own comfort when I perform by reproducing the way I want to feel physically in stressful situations. Its akin to being my own best friend. Out of respect for ourselves we can imagine a place where we feel we are wanted, needed, and respected. Perhaps you can recall a family gathering or a friends party where you were asked, no begged, to perform. Remember how it felt to be in demand, where any quality of performance would have been super to that audience. This feeling must be brought into the screen of our inner eye in full spectrum color, bright and clear, and made to fill us with its positive power. Sustaining the feeling from that warm image gives us a vehicle for comfort and enjoyment when one is not so apparent.

Being able to relax your muscles at will is something professionals have to do all the time. Whether we use images of water filling and emptying our tight and sore neck muscles until they loosen, or of a warm bath taking out those knots, we need one trick or another to keep us from suffering.

The foods we eat can also have an effect on the way we perform. The three main dishes that my colleagues and I typically eat before a performance are cheese omelets, fish, or chicken. These entrees sustain energy for hours and don't upset the stomach. As side dishes I include some of the following: broccoli, Brussel sprouts, celery, cucumbers, cabbage, carrots, bananas, dried fruit, grapes, dates, oranges, apples, blueberries, spinach, lettuce, tomatos, mushrooms, granola with yogurt, beans, or potato's. Having a big gooey dessert with mounds of sugar is strongly discouraged.

I never go to an audition without an "audition bag". In it I have high energy foods so that I'm prepared if called on to play another round. Usually you are notified a half hour or so before the next round begins. Such protein-filled items include bananas, hard-boiled eggs, raisins, yogurt, granola, fruit juice, and a peanut butter and jelly sandwich, (I never indulge in caffeinated beverages, chocolate or high sugar snacks). You may be able to feel the fruit juice give you a burst of energy within 5 minutes time, although most of the other foods take 20 minutes to be absorbed into your system enough to yield the feeling of additional power and energy. Two good food supplements include Lecithin and Enchinacea root drops (the latter being a chinese herb that boosts the immune system).

As a performer and teacher, I am constantly wrestling with the question of how to learn and expand. The challenge of expanding the creative possibilities in my art is what keeps me coming back to it. Discovering what information makes my students grow, and how to teach the knowledge to them in a way they will understand, is another rewarding challenge. Many times it is the self-criticism, self-consciousness, or fear that stops them from filling out their potential. Often I have to teach them how to use their brains.

The realization that the brain is an organ (like the heart or the kidney), apart from our spritual self, frees us to use it as a tool for our own benefit. We must stand apart from thinking that the brain is "ME". Thoughts are the automatic product of the brain's function. Seeing thinking as a process of that organ, like the heart pumping blood, we then can choose to view worry as the creative imagination seeing the worse outcome in a situation, or to use that creative energy to simply picture a positive outcome in that same situation. The latter frees us from fear and allows us to open us up to be our best. We can choose to watch our thoughts without reacting to them, or we can be at thier command no matter what they ask of us. To learn to ignore those voices that pop up and sabotage me, I've learned to let the thought happen, watch it as it swirls around inside, and finally let it pass out the top of my head. I don't listen to unhealthy thoughts but I respect those voices that care for me.

I direct my thinking toward the healthier perspectives of curiosity, understanding and humor instead of the destructive devices of self-criticism and self-consciousness. This helps me gain an objective stance over the emotional bias of stress. This helps me maintain grace and dignity when life seems to be falling apart. In this way I'm free to act, mold, and create instead of reacting to my defenses and falling back on past patterns of survival.

I have learned that the mind can only think one thought at a time. When it is not occupied with a thought, automatic, pre-determined and critical notions pop in to fill the void. One has to use the mind for the health of the body and spirit, or the idle thoughts of the unconscious take over. The chapter on self-talk explores ways of gaining control over the brain.

I often feel alienated when I perform with a new orchestra or in a new concert hall with its unknown acoustics. Creating a pleasant scenario at such times is imperative in order to perform without being self-conscious. Being surrounded by a loving and nurturing world is certainly desirable to me when I perform. It may or may not be true, I will never really know, but I've been told that the outside world is usually neutral; it does not really care one way or the other how well I do. It is just as easy to assume people like us than dislike us. Artists need to feel they are needed and respected in order to continue to perform every day under pressure. Unfortunately you can not expect to get positive feedback all the time or from everyone. It is part of my personal performing ritual to get in the frame of mind which allows me to be me. As positive-thinking, success-picturing athletes know, "psyching yourself up" before an event can give you the positive power needed to meet or perhaps exceed your previously established limits. Picturing yourself performing with confidence and relaxed assurance creates the type of environment in which you have a chance do your best.

The Stanislavski acting method gives us many techniques for believing in something imaginary. Pretending you are your favorite performer takes you outside of yourself so you can act like someone else. This reorientation of behavior is quite effective if you can act the part with all the particular nuances of the personality being copied. Act, don't react to circumstance.

I find it very necessary to stand apart from my work with my real self. I try to look down at the goings on at audition time and to be very removed emotionally. Dredging up cruel pictures of others performing our dreaded passages better than we think we can will sap the energy and confidence out of us. Being removed emotionally gives me perspective and sets up a chance to re-think the situation in order to turn it into a more enjoyable light. It presents me with a blank screen where I can then fill with the image I need to function the best. When I'm there in this twilight state I can change my outlook by reorienting my viewpoint with mood-altering images that are meaningful and powerful to me.

If for a moment I sense that I am stuck in a stressful situation, I feel out of control, with no options and no way out. At these times I use my rational-creative mind to acknowlege that I am, in fact, not stuck, and that I will come up with new and intriguing ways to make the situation different. It seems that artists in general know that they can change and mold their environments.

Treating ourselves with respect and love is hard for us as artists for it is easier to constantly be critical of ourselves in order to attain that goal of constantly improving as a performer. Splitting ourselves into two people, the sensitive, creative, child-artist, and the rational, parent, adult-king, is a practice that creates the space to change perspectives. I have found that dividing myself up into two persons each with different characteristics is quite natural. I come from a mother who is tremendously creative and emotional, and a father who is intensely cerebral and knowledgeable. I always score evenly on those left-brain-right-brain tests. The right-brained artistic, intuitive, and emotional self likes to dance and cajole around my logically controlled and opinionated left-brain self. Usually I allow and depend on my rational side to take charge and be the adult-parent, and cherish thoses infrequent occasions when I let my child out to play and wreck havoc upon the community.

I am very aware of burn out; how rejection, failure and criticism can take its toll. The perspective I take is to constantly remind myself that I will always receive more pleasure from the music than the profession takes out of me. Often the negative aspects of the profession wear me down, such as when a new person in town takes over work that I had done for years, or when a conductor tries to change my style, or when a colleague gives me the "wrong" feedback, or even excessive self-criticism. Sometimes I need to step back, perhaps take an entire summer off, and remember what I love about music and my instrument. It is during a hiatus that I relive my best moments of performing and the high points of my career. I discover once again the fulfillment and happiness music gives me and how it fills me with a sense of wonder and beauty. A break from performing "leads" me to new pathways and dimensions that perhaps no one has seen before. I become a mystic; poets and artists create our cultural life while in this state. Change is brought about by the dreamers. It is comforting to know that burnout can be remedied by love.

When we are nervous we are excessively monitoring our inner sensations and thoughts. This disrupts our concentration and flow. By using certain biofeedback techniques, we can shift our focus of attention to the external world where it belongs. I recently used an exercise in such techniques with a student who was so afraid of a difficult passage that she was not able to play through it, except when alone in the practice room. She had convinced herself that she would never be able to play it and how this was a pattern in her life and that there was no way she could ever have a career in music. Her distorted thinking was stopping her from functioning. In order to stop her destructive self-abuse, I took my reed knife and tapped it on the wall immediately behind her. I told her to keep her attention on the sharp blade of the knife, as she could not see it and was not sure what I was going to do with it. When she played the passage while thinking about the knife and the tapping, her technique was flawless. I explained to my awe-struck student that by turning her focus of attention from her self-talk, she was free to perform up to her natural abilities.

This focus could be anything that brings your attention, thoughts, feelings, or physical sensations away from previous negative behavior. One of my favorite techniques which is simple to do is to place your attention on the feel of your instrument. By touching the keys or fingerboard you can describe the texture, temperature, resistance, etc... so as to make your mind think of what you want it to rather than letting those automatic negative thoughts take over.

Biofeedback technicians use the terms *open* and *closed focus*. *Open focus* refers to the act of placing one's attention on things around or outside of the self. *Closed focus* describes the awareness of psychological goings on such as terrifying thoughts, (i.e., vague feelings of doom) as well as the physiological, (i.e., stomach pains, jolts from adrenalin, dizziness, shaking, sweating, etc...).

Our minds can be controlled by creatively juxtaposing physical, mental and emotional points of focus. The knife lesson was an example of physically focusing. We can amuse ourselves by placing our thoughts on objects and events surrounding us such as the floor, stage, chairs, windows, the temperature of the lights on your skin, the fly buzzing around, the cat hair on the conductor's sleeve, the smell of perfume wafting through your section, the sound of someone clearing their throat, the memory of how your last meat tasted, or any other zany things which come to mind. Still another way to focus is to get in an overall relaxed emotional state through meditative breathing which slows down mental and bodily rhythms. Mentally focusing on positive coping statements is another way to control your mind and will be discussed in great depth later on.

How do we know we are ready to play that first note? When do we give ourself the permission to begin to play? Actors have a good grasp on this problem. They believe that once they know the subtext, the underlying emotion, they can then deliver their lines. When performing I first establish in my mind the character of the phrase, then I set the correct tempo, and I'm off! During that moment of silence, when the expectation of the audience or audition committee fills the air, we can look forward to breaking the void with our song. A successful delivery is more assured when we first go through our own individual steps of mental preparation before. Executing a phrase with confidence and conviction makes our performance magical.

In the following pages I offer answers by myself and others in learning how to have relaxed and confident auditions and performances.

INTRODUCTION

Performers experience a different stress before the auditioner, or "examiner," than the type of stress experienced before a live audience. When presenting a live concert, the performer, in a sense, has invited the listener to enjoy the music as it becomes a mutual experience; a learning experience. The audience is, so to speak, on the side of the performer; it is rooting for him. In an audition, however, the atmosphere can be one of hostile competition.

Auditions are known for being a stressful ordeal. I have found, though, that there are people who are not affected by the pressure of auditioning as others are. In my own surveying of musicians, I found that approximately 70% have a harder time with nervousness and controlling anxiety at auditions than in performance. The remaining 30% function well at auditions and suffer more in performance.

I wondered why this 30% was able to view an audition without terror, and began asking to what they attributed this healthy attitude. These people generally were in touch with those feelings that put the audition process in perspective. They felt no threat to their self-esteem when faced with rejection, failure, competition, and jealousy. Whether this is a result of a "normal, healthy" upbringing, or simply of having a mature perspective on the music business, is hard to determine without going into an involved survey. Such is not the purpose of this book. Rather, its purpose is to help musicians deal with the audition from their own perspective and individual problems.

This book is organized into four broad areas which I felt covered the main problems that a person must face and come to terms with at an audition. First, the psychological adaptations to the stresses encountered: this includes understanding how the "self" operates; the pressures encountered; the individual fears experienced; the physical stress and its accompanying tension; the expectations of others and of ourselves; and finally, the self-consciousness that is often so distracting. Second, the reality of the music business itself: this includes how a person deals with criticism, failure, and jealousy and how a person relates his worth to the work he does. Third, coping techniques and strategies: this shows how a person prepares for the performance; deals with his feelings; how he talks to himself; ways of concentration; how he relaxes; how he uses humor as an outlet; what he eats and what drugs are taken. Fourth, successful outlooks and attitudes for auditioning: this includes ways of building confidence; ways of viewing an audition in a different way than as a trauma; and how a person can use his unique individuality to give strength and power to his performance.

In trying to share with others methods of dealing with the pressures of auditioning, I attempt to answer the many questions that need to be addressed. I hope that others will find this a tool to help them learn about dealing with the stress of auditioning and to get in touch with the power that is within them.

Author's note: I try not to be sexist; however I am using the masculine reference, with no discrimination intended. I find that the use of "his/her" every time the pronoun is needed is inefficient.

THE AUDITION PROCESS
ANXIETY MANAGEMENT AND COPING STRATEGIES

Chapter I

PSYCHOLOGICAL ADAPTATIONS TO AUDITION STRESSES

THE AUDITION RISK

It is possible for the auditioner to get himself into such a healthy frame of mind that he enjoys auditioning. It gives him a chance to show his stuff, to practice his craft, to give himself a high feeling, to experience and take a risk, and to meet a new challenge.[1]

It is important to keep in mind the idea that the audition committee on the other side of the desk is not engaged in some kind of conspiracy to keep you from getting the position, but rather is looking for the right person just as hard as you are looking for a job.[2] What the members are looking for is someone very interesting and talented as shown through each and every piece performed.[3]

The first principle of cognitive therapy is that ALL your moods are created by your cognitions or thoughts. This principle is useful if a performer is to understand how his mind works and feel in control of a situation. A cognition refers to the way you look at things; that is, your perceptions, mental attitudes, and beliefs. This includes the way you interpret things, revealed by what you say about something or someone to yourself. You FEEL the way you do right now because of the thoughts you are thinking at this moment.

The second principle of cognitive therapy is that when you are feeling depressed, your thoughts are dominated by a pervasive negativity that colors everything as hopeless.[4] Having bad thoughts and feelings usually results in feelings of inferiority which originate not so much from the "facts" or "experiences" themselves but from

[1]Michael Shurtleff, *Audition* (New York: Bantam Books, 1978) 31.
[2]Katinka Matson, *The Working Actor* (Canada: The Viking Press, 1976) 100.
[3]Shurtleff, op. cit., 13.
[4]David Burns, *The New Mood Therapy* (New York: The New American Library, Inc., 1980) 11.

1

our EVALUATION of these experiences. This feeling of inferiority comes about for one reason: we judge ourselves, and measure ourselves not against OUR "norm" or "par" but against some other individual's "norm". When we do this, we always, without exception, come out second best. The next conclusion is that we are not "worthy"; that we do not deserve success and happiness. In this frame of mind we feel that it would be out of place for us to fully express our own abilities and talents, whatever they might be, without apology or without feeling guilty about them. The opposite side of the coin is striving for superiority. This always leads to frustration and it seems that the harder we try, the more miserable we become.

Inferiority and superiority are the reverse sides of the same coin. The cure lies in realizing that the coin itself is spurious. The truth is that you are neither "inferior" or "superior." You are simply "you." You as a personality are not in competition with any other personality simply because there is no person on the face of the earth like you, or in your particular class. You are an individual.[5]

If your life is ever going to get better, you will have to take risks. There is simply no way you can grow without taking chances. Often, people become inhibited by fear at the very moment they must commit themselves to action. At the first sign of a reversal they doubt themselves, hesitate and, fearing that the situation is about to fall apart, retreat untested, convinced that they were in over their heads. They then feel thankful to have escaped. They do not understand that taking risks exceeds one's usual limits in reaching for any goal, and that uncertainty and danger are simply part of the process.[6]

To audition is to take a risk and to loosen your grip on the known and certain and to reach for something you are not entirely sure of but for what you believe is better than what you have now, or is at least necessary to survive.[7] You are the way you feel, and if you are unhappy in your present position, you have to do something to make it better. Therefore, the first risk you must take is to admit that you are not where you want to be and that you are not feeling the way you think you should feel. Admit it: you are basically just not happy.[8]

---

[5]Maxwell Maltz, *Psycho-Cybernetics* (New York: Prentice-Hall, 1960) 56.
[6]David Viscott, *Risking* (New York: Pocket Books, 1977) 13.
[7]Ibid., 17.
[8]Ibid., 31.

Committing to risk involves a willingness to accept responsibility for a loss. Accepting responsibility means that you are either going to do what has to be done or you are NOT going to do what has to be done. It follows then, that whatever happens, good or bad, it is either to your credit or it is your fault.[9] People who have difficulty taking risks want to know the outcome beforehand. This stems from an intense need to control events and this attitude, more than any action, causes the failure many dread so much.[10]

Risks involving self-esteem are always anxiety-provoking, for more than any other risk they seek to answer the question, "Am I good enough at what is most important to me?" And that alone is enough to stop many people (auditioners) in their tracks.[11]

There is nothing so difficult as putting your best on the line, except perhaps to yearn for successes that never happened because you were afraid to risk. A risk of esteem is successful when you simply put yourself on the line, do your best and accept your performance as an honest reflection of yourself. There will always be some part of your performance that is not perfect. You will always make some mistakes, no matter how extensive your preparation. A successful risk of esteem makes you more willing to risk the next time because you have overcome your hesitation to be yourself. When you try your best each succeeding risk can borrow some momentum from the risks taken before. When risks of esteem are successful your best self emerges. With this success your goals become clearer and you live your life simply by being you.[12]

There is some consolation in realizing that the risk-taking process is the same for everyone. No matter where you go, there is for the performer one moment when he must stand up alone in front of someone else and demonstrate his ability. This is an audition.[13]

You are sitting on a hard metal chair in some hallway or waiting room. Your palms sweat. Your heartbeat has increased by a third. Pangs of fear fly across your chest, down your stomach and back up your chest again. Your mouth is dry. Your hands shake, and when you stand your knees tremble. Breath is short. You sweat. Your mind

[9]Ibid., 123.
[10]Ibid., 180.
[11]Ibid., 196.
[12]Ibid., 201.
[13]Gordon Hunt, *How to Audition* (New York: Harper and Row, 1977) 51.

clouds over. For all you care, your life could end at that moment, and no one, especially you, would mind too much. As a matter of fact, death might be a blessed relief. The above is not a Prisoner of War about to undergo interrogation or a patient waiting for a life or death diagnosis, it is anyone who is about to go though that agonizing process known as the audition.[14]

All forms of competition are hostile. They may seem friendly on the surface but the prime motivation is to be or do "better than" anyone else. Although it may appear that the world is a competitive place, it is only competitive to those who feel the need to compete. Most people will reject this idea because of their childhood training where competition was rated right up there with apple pie and the American flag. If you ask them if they think competition is healthy, they will reply, with great enthusiasm, that it is not only healthy but necessary! They feel that it gives life meaning, purpose and direction; that a person needs a reward for doing a "good job." It never occurs to them that the reward is in the doing and not in the end result.[15]

The terror of having to put oneself on the line and face rejection can cause mental distress varying from mild stagefright to total emotional and physical collapse. Some performers give up in despair and vow never to be put in that thankless position again, while a few individuals cannot wait for the chance to show off their talents, skills, and hard work.[16]

What is there about the musical audition that makes it such a fearful prospect? Why are auditions necessary in the theatrical scheme of things? These questions have been haunting musicians and actors for ages.

The American Heritage Dictionary of the English Language defines an audition as "a presentation of something heard; a hearing, especially a trial hearing as that of an actor or musician." Obviously, we do not take that definition literally. If we did, auditioning over the telephone would be the norm rather than the exception. An audition is so much more than a hearing. It is really more like a one-sided job

---

[14]Ibid, 1.

[15]Robert Anthony, *Total Self-Confidence* (San Diego: Berkley Publishing Group, 1979) 25.

[16]Fred Silver, *Auditioning for the Musical Theatre* (New York: Newmarket Press, 1985) 13.

interview in that the auditors, are allowed to ask anything within reason of you, but you are not allowed the same privilege.[17]

Webster defines an audition as: "A trial performance to appraise an entertainer's merits." The words "trial" and "appraise" bring up connotations of terror. Is that what an audition is? A test of survival? For some it is. But if that is the case, your audition will suffer.[18]

A good audition may be one that gets the job, yet the real frustration lies in those many instances where brilliant auditions do not result in employment. Also discouraging are those instances where people with minimal talent get the job because they audition well, while those who are really gifted are just not that great at auditions. As mentioned before, we have unfortunately been brought up in a competitive society, where since kindergarten we have been taught that being first and being best are everything. Although this may apply to games on the playing field, it does not apply in the theatre and orchestra. Here, rather, actors and musicians are hired because they are right for an individual part. We are all individuals with our own specific talents. Success is so unpredictable; everyone has seen someone he feels is "less qualified" get the job he thought he should have gotten.[19]

Why do people put themselves through tortures like these? Money and fame are part of it, but the main reason is that they want to perform. They have a desire to stand up in front of their fellow human beings and attempt to portray or communicate something above, beyond, or just plain different from ordinary day to day communications. Why do some people have a desire to perform? The reasons are as varied as the number of people who do it. One person may have a violent need to be rejected, and so will constantly audition with just enough chip on his shoulder that, though he wins the audition, the group just does not want him around. Another might want to relive those shining moments of praise received from a parent, while another might think it is a good way to meet that needed mate.

[17]Ibid., 14.
[18]Hunt, op. cit., 51.
[19]Ibid., 18.

A person with healthy self-esteem derives great pleasure and pride from a creative existence to which he can bring all of his intellectual and emotional life to bear. What he seeks are means to express and objectify his self-esteem.[20] Whatever the reasons are on the surface there seems to be an even more fundamental reason why people go through this agonizing, blissful torture of auditioning. The gifted performer experiences sudden intuitive flashes in which insight "just comes." This mystical force releases momentary genius which the performer yearns to recreate in his artistic life.[21]

There are times when one's mind and emotions are not instantly and perfectly synchronized: he experiences desires or fears that clash with his rational understanding, and he must choose to follow either his rational understanding or his emotions. One of the most important things a child must learn is that emotions are not adequate guides to action. The fact that he fears to perform some action is not proof that he should avoid performing it.[22] When auditioning, it is hard not to trust your feelings about the situation and people.

There is a big difference between feeling victimized when auditioning, thereby allowing the judges their reality, and at the same time maintaining your own. You can never be the cause of anything unless you are also willing to be the effect of it. Do you resent the conductor, or perhaps the audition committee? Below are some obvious feelings one may have toward the audition or the audition givers, or both, as suggested by Gordon Hunt in his book, *How to Audition.*

a. Hostility: Many performers have some hostility towards the audition system and its personification, the person for whom they are auditioning. Perhaps thoughts like these run through your head : "Look at you sitting there. Who do you think you are judging me? Look at that stupid grin on your face. What's so funny? You think it's so easy to get up here and do this, you try it sometime instead of sitting there with that self-satisfied look on your face."

---

[20]Nathaniel Branden, *The Psychology of Self-Esteem* (New York: Bantam Books, 1981) 146.
[21]Ibid., 2.
[22]Ibid, 117.

b. Resentment: This is a slow-burning version of the above. It may be the result of many rejections, and it may be an overall feeling the performer, consciously or sub-consciously, carries around all the time. It can show in many ways: you may thereby hold back and not give your all; your attempts at humor are underscored with sarcasm; or you may have an overall negative or non-enthusiastic attitude.

c. Bluff: The "I'll show them a thing or two" approach. This is usually evidenced by a forced haughtiness, a "pushed" audition, and a facade of stardom or virtuosity which does not let anyone see the human being underneath.

d. Fear: This is the most prevalent negative feeling during an audition and is the real cause of all the feelings listed above.

Webster defines fear as: "An unpleasant, often strong, emotion caused by anticipation or awareness of danger." Fear is known as a physical, mental and emotional jolt which serves as a radar-like warning system when we feel our lives or just our security threatened. Feeling threatened is the product of our nerves being strung taut from laying ourselves open, naked, alone and defenseless to some kind of horrible fate. The feeling of fear is not a figment of the imagination, but a fear based on reality–a resimulation of past events. Fear which overwhelms the performer is, if traced back to its most basic elements, a very real concern of survival pure and simple. When placed in the solo spot we often become afraid for our lives on a purely emotional level. Although we know intellectually that this audition will be over soon and we'll walk out on the street and resume our lives again, we still have to prove ourselves, with no other support system than our own talent, instrument, body and presence. Unfortunately, this is often equated with some terrifying, lethal result.[23] Adapting to the psychological pressures often felt at auditions takes a combination of experience and insight. Accepting those negative feelings that appear can be the first step toward being able to function at ease. Taking an audition is to risk one's self-esteem. Sometimes a person may be resilient, yet at another audition that same individual may experience psychological damage so great that he will never take another. Understanding oneself is an extremely important part of the puzzle in being able to handle the pressures of auditioning.

[23]Hunt, op. cit., 54.

THE SELF AND ITS MANY PARTS

The biological function of the mind is COGNITION, EVALUATION, AND THE REGULATION OF ACTION. Since man must act he must apprehend reality accurately by relying on the aid of awareness and a knowlege of the facts. The crucial link between cognition and the regulation of action is EVALUATION. Evaluations are the basic ingredients underlying desires, emotions, and goals. This is important in order for a person to determine what is for him or against him.[24] These perceptions, then, will become important in the way he views auditioning.

Emotions reflect evaluations and interpretations; inappropriate or disturbed emotions proceed from inappropriate or disturbed judgements. These in turn proceed from inadequate or disturbed thinking.[25]

In trying to understand our SELF and how to use "it" effectively and efficiently, it is important to see how each part of the mind operates. Perhaps the most important aspect of the mind for this study is CONSCIOUSNESS. In his model of the human personality, Roberto Assagiolo adapted a school of philosophy called "psychosynthesis." In it he describes the hierarchy of consciousness:

1. The Lower Unconscious

2. The Middle Unconscious

3. The Higher Unconscious or Superconscious

4. The Field of Consciousness

5. The Conscious Self or "I"

6. The Higher Self

The Lower Unconscious contains prime instincts, directed mainly at self-preservation. This can stimulate the feeling of stagefright if these instincts remain outside our awareness. The Higher Unconscious, which contains the Higher Self, gives us ideas, insights, intuition, and allows us to make hunches.

---

[24]Branden, op. cit., 1981) 97.
[25]Ibid. 103.

What interests us is the middle level, the mediator of the two. In order for the energies of the lower level to be transformed and those of the upper level to be manifested, they must be brought into the middle area of conscious awareness. This is where thoughts take place.[26] When we experience our thoughts, we experience ourselves. When we use the word "I," we are saying that we recognize someone as being "ourself." Without realizing it, we experience this combination of body, name, thoughts, feelings, and memories and call it "me." If we believe or act as though this collection of factors is all there is to us, however, we are missing something. There is also an Observer in us that views everything going on in our body, heart, and mind. This is the part that is always watching us do what we do, seeing all of our circumstances from a broad perspective. "This is different from the Object Self–the collection of 'me-identifying factors'" that was just mentioned (our body, name, thoughts, feelings, and memories).[27]

This knowledge is particulary valuable in dealing with the upsets of auditioning. Rather than suffer through an endless succession of mental and emotional traumas, you can see your life from the viewpoint of an objective observer rather than that of a frazzled participant. Clear observation enables you to see things as they are, to notice which factors can be changed, and which must be changed, in order to get through this crisis. Then you can act firmly and appropriately. Switching to the observer's point of view takes you out of the whirl of circumstances and gives you balance.

The OBJECT SELF/OBSERVER distinction is helpful in discussing issues of control and surrender. If we believe that the object-self is all there is to this person we call "me," then the prospect of surrender (to failure or whatever) may seem frightening. However, when we realize that we are more than we may have given ourselves credit for, that someone would remain if we did "surrender" or let go of a particular thought, feeling, or situation, then the prospect of letting go seems less fearsome.[28] In his book, *The Inner Game of Music*, Barry Green describes the self as being divided up into two parts: Self 1 and Self 2. Self 1 is our interference, containing our concepts of how things should be, our judgments and our associations. It favors the

---

[26]Robert Triplett, *Stage-fright: Letting It Work For You* (Chicago: Nelson-Hall, 1983) 21.

[27]Elizabeth Brenner, *Winning by Letting Go* (San Diego: Harcourt Brace Jovanovich, 1985) 6-7.

[28]Ibid. 7.

words "should" and "shouldn't," and often sees things in terms of what "could have been." Self 1 talks to us of the past and the future and loves to predict upcoming failures and successes. It considers things that have already happened with the words, "if only." Self 1 includes not only our own thoughts, but also whatever we have picked up from our teacher's instructions, our friends's suggestions, our parents's hopes and desires, and our own urge to fulfill or reject those expectations. It includes everything we "think" we should be doing or about what we should be worrying.

Self 2 is a vast reservoir of potential we each have. It contains our natural talents and abilities, and is a nearly unlimited resource to tap and develop. Left to its own devices it performs with gracefulness and ease.[29] Self 2 is an "unthinking" state, one in which we are both relaxed and aware. Through it we are letting our true ability and musicality express itself, without control or manipulation.

Green goes on to explain how best to handle the chatter of self 1. He states that thinking is natural, and thoughts are likely to be present in every aspect of our lives; sometimes we pay attention to our thoughts and sometimes we ignore them and change the subject. It is helpful to notice our thoughts, for then we can determine how much they contribute to our activity and how much they interfere with it. We can opt to ignore the "good advice of Self1." We do not have to give in to our natural tendency to talk back to Self 1. Not only is Self 1 talking to us, but our own response is getting in our way of concentrating on the audition. Rather, it is more advantageous to focus on something that is happening right now, in the present moment. When we choose not to listen in on these voices, we eliminate our doubts and fears simply by ignoring them.

In understanding how the mind works, we see that we have automatic thoughts that enter our consciousness at will. We also notice that chattering voices have subpersonalities. In his book, *StageFright*, Robert Triplett notes that these thought patterns on issues relating to fear or stagefright center around three issues: DOUBT, CRITICISM, AND FEAR. These subpersonalities and how they are central to breaking through the problems we face at an audition will be discussed at length later on in this book.

---

[29]Barry Green, *The Inner Game of Music* (New York: Anchor Press, 1986) 16-21.
[30]Ibid., 15.

PSYCHOLOGICAL PRESSURES

When preparing for an audition there are varied pressures that may affect a person. Besides the physical tension ("to be discussed later), the mental workings become emeshed in confusion and doubt. With the realization of an impending audition, it is amazing how suddenly nervousness, worry, and issues of self-esteem seem to crop up.

In his book, *The Inner Game of Music*, Barry Green cites a list of mental problems different individuals have encountered when under pressure. They include:

1. Doubting their ability;

2. Being afraid of losing control;

3. Feeling they had not practiced enough;

4. Being concerned they could not hear or see properly;

5. Having thoughts of equipment malfunction;

6. Worrying about losing their place in the music;

7. Doubting the audience would like their playing;

8. Having a fear of memory slips; and

9. General worry.[30]

WORRY

Usually the first thing a person notices is that he is worrying about the audition. This would include all the little details such as plane tickets, hotel reservations, preparing the materials, and perhaps some other secret issues. Learning to break the worry habit can take a great burden off the performer and should become a priority if worry tends to upset his performance. Here is a listing of what some experts have to say on the subject:

Merge Yourself with the Music

It is important to move toward a point where you are comfortable with the experience of YOURSELF IN THE ACT OF PLAYING SO

---

[31]Ibid. 64.

that your musical experience can come through. Getting rid of the interference that blocks your enjoyment helps you become the music.[31]

Worrying about Failing

Putting your attention on trusting yourself instead of on trying to lose your concentration on your awareness of things around you or on wild thoughts can help ease the worry of failing.[32] When we accept our role as interpreters of the composer's music, we cease to be so worried about how we appear to others.[33] Allowing yourself to fail is totally different from asking permission from others, because allowing yourself to fail opens up the possibility of allowing yourself to succeed.[34]

Looking for Other Options

When worrying about a situation, check what other alternatives are available, what the consequences would be, and how to limit the damage.[35]

Appreciate the Service You Are Providing

Serving people is the way to serve yourself.[36]

Picture Yourself Succeeding

Instead of worrying, relax the strain, stop trying to "do it" by strain and effort. Picture the target you really want to hit and let your creative success mechanism work for you and trust it. Mentally picturing the desired end result literally forces you to use positive thinking.[37]

---

[32]Ibid. 80.
[33]Ibid. 81.
[34]Triplett, op. cit., 176.
[35]Brenner, op. cit., 164.
[36]Ibid. 173.
[37]Maltz, op. cit., 41.

Change "What Might Happen" to What You Hope will Happen

Generate enough good emotional feelings and your pictured goal will become very vivid in your mind and create enthusiasm, encouragement, cheerfulness and a happy state.[38]

Keep Your Purpose In Mind

Try to rid yourself of "shadow talk," that is, negative self-criticism, by consciously keeping your main idea in your thoughts.[39]

Do Not Respond to Your Imagination

Because your nervous system cannot tell the difference between real experience and imagined ones, choose to ignore the "what ifs" and adverse mental pictures.[40]

Substitute Pleasant Images For Worry Images

Make a habit out of immediately inserting a pre-planned pleasant picture whenever you catch yourself worrying.[41]

Worry About a Positive Goal

If you have to worry, use your imagination to play out positive goals.[42]

Expending the Feeling

Concentrate on the worry and note what happens to your body as well as what thoughts and feelings bubble up. Relive the circumstances of the worry situation and make all the mistakes you can. Exaggerate every detail so that all aspects are clearly defined. Experience the feeling and let it expend itself. If the feelings become too overwhelming, ease away and relax.[43]

---

[38]Ibid. 74.
[39]Ibid. 173.
[40]Ibid. 200.
[41]Ibid. 239.
[42]Ibid. 234.
[43]Triplett, op. cit., 175.

Choosing to Perform Without Worry

If worry were gone, what feelings would you feel? What thoughts would you think and what would your body be like? Shift your body into this new position. Picture the way it would be if there were no worry. Would you perform with more energy, more intimacy, more looseness, or what? Perform as you imagine you could if the worry were dissolved. Act as if the worry no longer exists and begin to perform in a different way. Stop and relax.[44]

Living in the Here and Now

Keeping your thoughts in the present and do not let them wander to your past errors and future fears. This helps eliminate a lot of worries. and will help keep yourself open to the intuitive guidance from within. At the same time this will help you enjoy each step of your performance.[45]

Reverse, Not Rehearse, Your Failures

By giving your dominant thoughts over to failure, you are impelled to fail. Failure is rehearsed by constant repetition. Be mentally prepared should failure occur, yet have the confidence to enable you to meet and successfully handle these challenges. If you are able to stay in the present time zone, you can see that it is impossible to worry because absorption in the present moments blocks out other thoughts. The mind cannot think of two things at the same time.[46]

Keep Your Mind on the Rewards

To overcome apprehension, keep in mind the ultimate benefits you will receive. This helps you look at everything in your life as a chance to change for the better. Think of the possible positive consequences and look forward to the future instead of worrying about it.[47]

---

[44]Ibid. 176.
[45]Anthony, op. cit., 124.
[46]Ibid. 169
[47]Ibid. 173

DOUBT

When the pressures of an audition arise, the event is seen as a test situation and uncertainty begins to enter the mind. Questioning one's talents and abilities becomes almost an obsession if one is not able to subdue these thoughts. Here are some suggestions to help rid yourself of doubt.

Stay in the Present

The doubter is future oriented and constantly asks, "what if?"[48]

Center Your Attention

Find your focus by believing in your actions.

Feel Prepared and Find Your Enjoyment

Consider the possibility of believing in yourself.

Trust Your Abilities

Have faith in what you do and let go of rigid self-conscious control to let the natural mystery of the music unfold. Through trust we find singleness of purpose and our attention is pinpointed on our audition.[49]

Recognize a Conflict Between Values

Thoughts such as "I must," or "I cannot," show a conflict in what is considered important. It could be a standard, an expectation, a demand or a claim that a person believes is in his power to satisfy.[50]

WEAKNESS

When we take an audition many feelings come to the surface. From the doubt and worry come fear. Being afraid leaves a person feeling helpless and weak.

---

[48]Triplett, op. cit., 34.
[49]Ibid. 98-101.
[50]Branden, op. cit., 1981) 160.

The weakling part of ourself feels victimized, seeks strength wherever he can find it and seeks a protector who will have some "magic" powers to leave him unharmed. Because the weakling cannot find the answers to strengthen himself, each question is met with a claim of ignorance. This shield of ineptitude leaves him saying, "I don't know, because. . ." to the pressures of the performance.[51]

Along with feeling weak, other negative responses include: nervousness, control issues, power issues such as having to prove yourself, guilt, frustration, helplessness and hopelessness, feeling worthless, exposing yourself to risk and uncertainty, procrastination and depression. Below is a listing of problems and some insights into dealing with negative responses.

Fear Seeks Blind Confidence

The weakling seeks a protector to supply the strength needed. This protector is defensive and wants to show off his "magic answers". The weakling seeks domination by some outside power and gives up trying to find the needed courage.[52]

Fear Needs Courage

The weakling needs the energy of the risker. Without weakness there is nothing to risk, and without risk there is no perception of weakness. Weakness brings prudence and a measure of sensitivity, while the risker contributes the elements of thrill and adventure.[53]

Joy is the Reward

The energies of fear and courage interweave, producing joy. Since joy is the product of exploration, the discoverer strikes out on new paths by which we can approach our craft. We encounter both success and failure from which we glean valuable information important to our growth. In giving us new ideas with which to experiment, the discoverer offers us refreshment and vitality, and our performance is rejuvenated.[54]

---

[51]Ibid. 37-41.
[52]Ibid. 94.
[53]Ibid. 94.
[54]Ibid. 94

Allow Your Nerves to be There

When you feel any of the symptoms of anxiety or nervousness, DO NOT CRITICIZE YOURSELF. Just try and see how much you can notice about your present condition. Has putting your attention on the problem changed it? Give it permission to be there and then choose another focus for your attention.[55]

Relaxation Helps Conquer Helplessness

The ability to deliberately relax helps a person to feel he has some command over that which he fears.[56]

Fear of Losing Control

The fear of losing control is rooted in lack of trust in ourselves and the world around us. It can make us feel like helpless infants who have no control over the fundamentals of life. Successful people know that examining their fears helps them recover their basic trust and enables them to CHOOSE their response instead of reacting automatically to the promptings of their fears.[57]

Surrender Leads to Control

Control ("to make ourselves stop running from the voices in our heads) leads to surrender ("seeing what is already there) which leads to control ("not allowing the contents of our mind to dominate our behavior) which leads to surrender ("allowing an enjoyable audition).[58]

Making Nerves Work for You

If we can maintain an aggressive attitude, that is, react aggressively instead of negatively to threats and crisis, the very situation itself can act as a stimulus to release untapped powers. Think about what you are going to do and what you want to happen instead of what may happen or what you fear will happen.[59]

---

[55]Green, op. cit., 48
[56]Herbert Fensterheim, *Stop Running Scared!* (New York: Dell Publishing Co., Inc., 1977) 101.
[57]Brenner, op. cit., 35.
[58]Ibid. 198.
[59]Maltz, op. cit., 215.

Use Your Imagination and Picture Images of Strength

Building a heathy self-image requires using positive models.[60]

Procrastination is the Result of Self-Defeating Thoughts

Self-defeating thoughts lead to self-defeating emotions which lead to self-defeating actions which end up in a pattern of repetition.[61]

Mind-Sets Associated with Do-Nothingism

Hopelessness

Helplessness

Overwhelming yourself

Jumping to conclusions

Undervaluing the rewards

Perfectionism

Fear of failure

Fear of success

Fear of disapproval or criticism

Coercion or resentment

Low frustration tolerance

Guilt and self-blame

Depression

There is a distinction between sadness and depression. Sadness is a normal emotion created by realistic perceptions that describe a negative event involving a loss or disappointment in an undistorted way. Depression is an illness that always results from thoughts that are distorted in some way.[62]

Depression can be Dangerous

There are different degrees of depression ranging from a case of the blues to suicide. Talking to a friend or a professional can relieve the pressure built up from the effects of an audition.

[60]Ibid. 31.

[61]David D. Burns, M.D., *Feeling Good* (New York: William Morrow and Co., Inc., 1980) 81.

[62]Ibid. 207

STRESS MANAGEMENT

Because the psychological pressures affect different people in different ways, it is good to know the various treatments offered, should a person want to explore them. Listed below are specific strategies which can help an otherwise prepared musician deal with anxiety thereby enabling him to play more comfortably and at a higher level of musical attainment.

ANXIETY. Chronic generalized anxiety ("trait) is stable over time and appears in a number of situations, while state anxiety may be brought on by specific situations and varies greatly over time. Strategies for management include: relaxation training, biofeedback, hypnosis, guided imagery, exercise, diet modification, and in more severe cases, drug or psychiatric therapy.

1. AUTOGENIC OR RELAXATION TRAINING. Autogenic training is systematic relaxation of muscle groups performed with either a prerecorded set of taped instructions or by systematically thinking the relaxation instructions. Deep breathing exercises are frequently included in these instructions. A principle advantage is that after a few weeks of practice one can relax specific muscle groups during a performance. When one is in a more relaxed state, respiration slows down and thereby mitigates the problems of racing heart rate and hyperventilation.

2. BIOFEEDBACK. Biofeedback is a system of electrical measurements in which electrodes are superficially attached to the skin to monitor activity in the muscle groups. The goal of this therapy is to make patients aware of physiologic responses, to enable them to gain control of these responses in a clinical setting, and to generalize this control into day-to-day adverse circumstances.

3. HYPNOSIS. A therapist gives general suggestions of peace and comfort or may deal with specific factors such as heart-rate, perspiration, note memory, anxiety level or any other factor that may be a problem.

4. IMAGERY. This therapy consists of imagining a specific pleasant, relaxed environment, such as a walk in the woods on

a sunny day. When the patient has reached a good state of relaxation and self-confidence, the therapist introduces a symbolic idea (a large tree, for example) representing a significant stressor, such as an upcoming audition. The patient is then guided as to how to perceive the tree (audition) in non-threatening terms and is given post- hypnotic suggestions which reinforce the gains in ego- strength made during the imagery.

5. DIET MODIFICATION. It is found that foods rich in the amino acid L-tryptophan can serve as a natural tranquilizer. These foods include milk, cheese, and dairy products. The elimination of coffee, tea, colas, chocolate and cigarettes can also relieve anxiety symptoms.

6. DRUG THERAPY. Anti-anxiety drugs carry with them the risk of addiction. In extreme cases, drugs can be beneficial. The use of Inderal has been tested specifically with a population of performing musicians and has shown to be effective.

7. PSYCHIATRIC/PSYCHOLOGICAL CARE. If performance stress is not responsive to one or several of the previously outlined therapies, it may be a trait anxiety and a symptom of more deeply rooted problems. Many musicians self-destruct and the historical literature is full of examples of musicians who could never quite cope with environmental and intrapersonal demands. Such persons are strongly urged to get mental health care from qualified personnel.[63]

In learning to deal with the psychological pressures of auditioning, it is helpful to know where to go to get the type of health care needed. Opposite is a chart which lists general information as to which medical specialty or paramedical profession is likely to be most beneficial.

---

[63]Marilyn Tuck, "Stress Management and Musical Performance," (*The American Organist* : 17:54-5 March 1983) 54-58.

THERAPY	SPECIALTY
Autogenic training	Psychology (Behavioral)
Biofeedback	Psychology (Behavioral)
Hypnosis and Guided Imagery	Anesthesia
	Counseling
	Psychology (Behavioral or Clinical)
	Social work
Exercise	Physical therapy
	Exercise physiology
Diet modifications	Nutrition
Drug therapy	Cardiology
	Internal medicine
	Psychiatry
Mental health care	Counseling
	Psychiatry
	Psychology ("Clinical)
	Social work

FEAR

The most prevalent negative feeling a person has during an audition is fear. Webster defines fear as: "An unpleasant, often strong emotion caused by anticipation or awareness of danger." We have come to know fear as a physical, mental, and emotional surge which provides us with a radar-like warning system when we feel our lives are threatened. Since this need is less evident in our day-to-day lives here in the twentieth century than it was in a wild environment from which we came, it is worth asking why this system operates just as strongly as if our lives were being threatened in situations which, if viewed objectively, did not really threaten our lives at all.

When fear fills your being as you go into an audition, your nerves are strung taut. These are not the normal feelings which accompany

21

an ordinary job-seeking situation. Why is it that a real blood and guts, live or die jungle battle happens in an audition? The reason is partly that when we audition, we often feel we are actually laying ourselves open, naked, alone and defenseless to some kind of horrible fate. The feeling of fear is not a figment of the imagination, but rather a fear based on reality; a reminder of past events. Some might call this reaction racial or genetic memory, whereas others would be more specific and say these events actually occured back in time. Either way, it is a very real fear for survival. When placed in that solo spot we often become literally afraid for our lives on a purely emotional level. Intellectually we realize this audition will soon be over, that we will walk out on the street and resume our lives again. But somehow having to PROVE OURSELVES, and revealing ourselves to others with nothing more supporting us than our own talent, voice, body and presence, is often mentally equated with a terrifying, perhaps lethal, result.

Here are a few examples of needless, yet painful fears experienced at auditions:

1. Being afraid they will say you are not good enough, and a rejection will reinforce your pattern of failure.

2. Being afraid of not reinforcing a pattern of failure by being accepted. If we are accepted we will no longer be able to retreat to this safe place of failure, but must begin to take a step toward self-reliance. This can be frightening enough to make us adopt a crippling fear which may then limit and often ruin an audition.

3. Being afraid of getting the job because you will then have to become an adult, and you are not ready for that.

4. Being afraid of getting the job because you know you are worthless and if you get the job, everyone else will know it too.

5. Being afraid if you give your all at this audition, you will uncover feelings of great joy, and if you do that you may be so disappointed when they go away that you could die.

6. If you give your all at this audition you are afraid of uncovering great feelings of sorrow because you could lose emotional control.

7. If you give your all at an audition, you are afraid of uncovering great hostilities. You could probably kill those judges out there who are putting you on the spot.

8. You are afraid the authority figure out there with the pad and pencil will not like you. How often do you think of that auditioner as a father image, judging you, praising or damning you, loving you, or not loving you? It is no wonder you get frightened. At the infantile level, parents' approval means survival. If they like you they feed and take care of you and you live. Many of us may continue to feel this way to one degree or another when we are called upon to please someone, as is required in an audition.[64]

Some nervousness is natural, but the fear that cripples us, that takes us out of the present time, and prevents us from really opening up and doing our best work, is what we want to discard. Naturally, the less fear, the better the audition. Here are some approaches to eliminate unnecessary fears from the audition situation.

Picture the Worst Thing That Can Happen

If you allow your imagination to run wild, chances are your fear will be traced somehow to some form of dying since that seems to be the ultimate fear of many. Even though you know you are nervous and not going to die, you still feel it. Feeling like you are going to die means that your subconscious mind links the audition experience with possible death, and that makes it seem that you are literally putting your life on the line. One way of temporarily short-circuiting this fear (so the audition becomes not a trial at which your life is at stake, but an experience where you can be free and creative and show the very best you have to offer) is to work out your fears beforehand until the immediate emotional impact is gone. Write them out, stare at them, feel the emotions and sensations that go with them until you have wrestled some of the bad feelings which plague you.

Get Yourself Out of the Way

When you feel overwhelming self-concern, you may feel as if you can only deal with yourself and nothing else. Try putting yourself into the world around you by using your senses to pick out sounds

---

[64]Hunt, op. cit., 54-56.

that you hear right now, in the present moment. Feel the temperature in the room, the clothes you are wearing, your instrument. Be aware of the taste in your mouth and how dry or damp it is. Instead of limiting your thoughts to only yourself and thus reducing the world to your size, open up and expand yourself to the size of the world.

Exercise

Get your blood flowing, your body moving and generally tone yourself up, as opposed to just slopping through, or allowing yourself to go in less than optimum condition. By exercising you are doing something positive toward getting that job, and you can carry the feeling that you have done all you can. This is one way of bringing a more positive, up feeling to the audition. Exercises like sit-ups, leg-raises, knee-bends, toe-raises, and perhaps some jogging, get you in control of your body instead of the other way around.

Deep Breathing

A few deep breaths from the lower part of the lungs help to get rid of tension, relax the body, and slow down the mind.

Make the Day Joyous

Plan a fun evening after the audition so there is something to which you can look forward. Help someone before you go to the audition, such as calling a friend who is in trouble to see how they are doing. Look around you at the audition and find something funny. Reaching outside of yourself will eliminate a lot of self-concern and it will make you feel like a giving, positive participant in life. Make up some things to make your day special and enjoyable.

Have Something Creative to Go To

Again, have a definite activity in mind after the audition so it is not the end of your day. Attend a movie, write a poem, or paint your apartment. Do something which involves some constructive activity, as opposed to destructive ones! This helps your mind dwell on something other than yourself, by taking all-important feelings off the audition.

Stay Off Drugs

Alcohol and drugs alter the consciousness. Your best work is done with a clear channel which is able to receive, absorb, and then return all creative energies, thoughts, feelings and ideas that come your way.

Get All the Information Possible

You will be calmer and feel more in control when you know the familar. Then, you will not have to worry about all the little things of which you are unsure. Know what is expected of you and prepare accordingly.[65]

Specific Fears

Each person has his own special fears. These fears range from a general fear of failure to a particular fear of dropping the instrument. These fears almost become phobia-like and can destroy concentration and one's obsessing on specific problems may actually prevent the taking of an audition. These fears fall into two categories: mental and physical.

Physical Problems Include:
  loss of breath
  dry mouth
  increased heartbeat
  sweaty hands
  shaking fingers, arms, or knees
  loss of ability to see or hear clearly
  tension
  stiff body movement
  feeling sick[66]
  getting dizzy

Mental Problems Include:
  inner voices blaming or praising
  forgetting the words or fingering
  forgetting the music
  losing the sense of timing
  feeling distracted

---

[65] Ibid. 56-67.
[66]Green, op. cit., 16.

25

losing concentration

being confused[67]

This list of specific fears can be expanded to include the type of interference each person fears. The following are examples of what some of these might be.

FEAR OF: darkness, sudden noises, fire, feeling angry, drugs, hurting others, being with people of the opposite sex, entering a room where people are already seated, being ignored, making mistakes, success, being trapped, high places, elevators, crowded places, new things, being a leader, arguing, tunnels, traveling alone, strange foods, strange people, driving a car, being punished by God, thoughts, closeness, losing control, other people being angry with you, fainting, dizziness, suffocating, missing a heartbeat, falling, large open places, crossing streets, blushing, being independent, accidents, spending money, losing a job, making decisions, being criticized, being watched, performing in public, bridges, leaving home, tests, being dressed unsuitably, tough-looking people, and being teased.[68]

Because of the different intensities of a fear reaction, it is beneficial to define different levels of fear. Herbert Fensterheim does so in his book entitled *Stop Running Scared!* as described below:

1. NORMAL FEAR can serve as a useful emotion. It can spur you on to take life-saving measures. It can sharpen your perceptions, mobilize your energies, and clarify your thoughts so you can perform better.

2. IRRATIONAL FEAR is caused when minimal or no danger exists, yet you act as if great peril were involved.

3. ANXIETY is an upsetting emotional state marked by continual fear or a feeling of threat. Often you cannot put into words what actually threatens you; you just feel nervous.

4. PHOBIA means a persistent fear of an object or idea that ordinarily does not justify fear. You know this is ridiculous but you cannot overcome it.

5. PANIC denotes a sudden surge of acute terror.[69]

---

[67]Ibid. 16.

[68]Fensterheim, op. cit., 54-55.

[69]Ibid. 28-29.

Fensterheim also categorizes the following five basic kinds of fears: fear of things and places (such as heights and snakes); interpersonal and social fears (such as rejection and failure); fear of internal fears (such as heart palpitations and dizziness); fear of thoughts (that intrude suddenly and bring about anxiety); deprivative fears (in which the actual fears are not the main problem).[70]

In order to change the fear behavior, two main goals must be kept in mind: 1. to be able to feel less frightened in the fear situation itself and 2. to carry out certain actions that will weaken your fear rather than strengthen it. There exists a fear trigger that sets off the fear reaction. The impetus may be your thoughts ("I'm sure I'm going to fail") or your reaction to your own internal sensations (like dizziness).[71]

There are seven ways in which to react to a fear situation: 1. to dodge it; 2. to run away; 3. to obsess on the worst possible consequence; 4. to manipulate people to keep the fear situation from arising; 5. to distort and rationalize your fear so it seems reasonable; 6. to refuse to cope because of focus on the feelings of fright; and 7. to suffer silently.

In order to learn to control your fear, Fensterheim says you must: 1. understand your nervous system from the mental to the physical; 2. understand how you learned your fears. Was it from bad experiences or that you saw someone else frightened?; 3. see how you keep your fear alive and how it influences your life-style and affects your behavior pattern; 4. realize the relationship between the intensity of your fear and your sense of self-command. You want to decrease the intensity of your fear and increase your self-command.[72]

Most fears associated with audition problems lie in the realm of social fears. These include:

1. A fear of being looked at.

2. A fear of people seeing that you are nervous, as it shows the outward manifestations of your symptom.

3. A fear of being trapped in an interpersonal relationship such as knowing you will have to talk with someone you do not want to meet.

[70]Ibid. 50-53.
[71]Ibid. 33.
[72]Ibid . 40-42.

4. A fear of being "found out," which implies that when people really know you, that is, if you are exposed for what you really are, they will reject you.

5. A fear of negative feelings such as anger and criticism from others or yourself, which can influence your whole life-style.

6. A fear of doing things alone, which may be connected to loneliness and depression.

7. A fear of not getting along with another. This involves issues of being ignored and a fear of a lull in the conversation.

Within this category are five special fears:

of not being liked
of looking foolish
of rejection
of inadvertently hurting others
of being wrong[73]

Given these perspectives in understanding fear, we will now consider some ways of thinking which may help to deal with fear and its symptoms.

DEALING WITH FEAR

Rational-Emotive therapist Albert Ellis talks about the control of anxiety and fear by "straight thinking," for anxiety consists of the irrational idea: "THAT IF SOMETHING SEEMS DANGEROUS OR FEAR-SOME, YOU MUST PREOCCUPY YOURSELF WITH AND MAKE YOUR-SELF ANXIOUS ABOUT IT."[74] Real and rational fears do exist and being concerned about your safety is a necessity for self-preservation. Anxiety or intense fear consists of OVERCONCERN, of EXAG-GERATED OR NEEDLESS fear. However, as it does not relate to physical injury or illness, it usually relates to OVERCONCERN FOR WHAT SOMEONE THINKS ABOUT YOU. Here are some reasons why exaggerated fear appears self-defeating:

---

[73]Ibid. 179-81.

[74]Albert Ellis, *A New Guide to Rational Living* (New Jersey: Prentice-Hall, Inc., 1975) pg 145.

1. If something is truly dangerous, you may take two intellegent approaches.

    A. determine whether this thing ACTUALLY involves danger

    B. if so, either do something practical to alleviate the danger, or resign yourself to the fact of its existence.

2. If something does happen, you can usually do nothing else about it. Worry has no magical quality to prevent bad luck but frequently increases the probability of it happening.

3. You exaggerate the assumed catastrophic quality of many potentially unpleasant events. If you accept reality and stop making up negative images in your head, you can accept the obvious fact that whatever exists exists, no matter how unpleasant and inconvienient you find the experience. Consequently, nothing will truly strike you as "awful," "horrible," or "terrible."

4. Worry itself develops into one of the most painful conditions.

5. Aside from the possibility of physical harm or acute deprivation, what can you really ever fear? So what if some people may disapprove or dislike you. As long as you do not literally suffer, why give yourself a super-hard time about the wheels that turn in your head? If you stop worrying and do something about avoiding a possible disapproval, you will probably counteract it. If you can do nothing about it; tough again! but do not stew.

6. Realize that you have more control as an adult than you did as a child who has little or no control over his destiny.[75]

COUNTERATTACKS AGAINST INAPPROPRIATE ANXIETIES

1. Track your worries and fears back to the specific belief of which they consist. How awful or terrible is it?

2. When a situation actually involves danger, you can sensibly

[75]Ibid. 144-46.

29

    A. change the situation or

    B. accept the danger as one of the unfortunate facts of life. No matter what, the inevitable remains inevitable; and no amount of worrying will make it less so.

3. If a dire event may occur, and you can do no more to ward it off, then realistically weigh the chances of its occuring and realistically assess the consequences of its occurrence.

4. Realize that you created the anxiety by your internal sentences; so challenge and dispute them.

5. Most anxieties related to the dread of making public mistakes, antagonizing others, or of losing love relate back to a fear of disapproval.

6. Realize that worry will aggravate rather than improve the situation.

7. Try not to exaggerate the importance or significance of things.

8. Distraction may temporarily dissipate groundless fear. Focus on the content of what you are doing instead of your thoughts and symptoms.

9. Track down your present fears to their earlier origins and realize how they once seemed fairly appropriate but how they no longer hold water.

10. Do not be ashamed of anxieties which continue to exist. Admit that you feel needlessly fearful. Do not degrade yourself for making yourself anxious.

11. Do not be surprised if your anxieties come back from time to time.[76]

Successful people know that examining fears helps them recover their basic trust and enables them to choose responses instead of reacting automatically to the promptings of their unconscious fears.[77] It is important to experience the fear and then let it go. Elizabeth Brenner suggests the following steps to overcome fear:

---

[76]Ibid. 155-57.
[77]Brenner, op. cit., 35.

1. OBSERVE AND CLEARLY ACKNOWLEDGE IT. The experience may take the form of trembling and nausea, of emotional sensations, or of mental images. Whatever form it takes, if we allow it to come over us it will pass much more quickly than we anticipated.

2. OBSERVE HOW MANY THINGS IN NATURE AND LIFE ACTUALLY DO WORK OUT. As we align ourselves with the positive side of the universe, we diminish our need to cling to our fears.

3. NOTICE THE FEAR AND LET IT BE THERE, YET SURRENDER ANYWAY.[78]

4. SEE WHAT WE CAN CONTROL AND WHAT WE CANNOT.

5. WE OUGHT NOT TO BECOME ATTACHED ABOUT THE RESULTS OF OUR ACTIONS.

6. SURRENDER TO YOUR FEAR WITH GRACE AND CHOOSE LIFE- SERVING OVER LIFE-NEGATING SURRENDERS.[79]

Maxwell Maltz suggests these approaches in his book, *Psychocybernetics*:

1. If you are fearful in a situation, see yourself acting calmly and deliberately, with confidence, courage and expansive feelings. This builds up memories and stored data and helps build a new self-image. After awhile you will not have to think about it or try to make an effort.[80]

2. Once a decision is reached and execution is the order of the day, dismiss absolutely all responsibility and care about the outcome. Unclamp your intellectual and practical machinery and let it run free.[81]

3. The feeling of fear does not represent the truth about a future event, but about your own attitude of mind within you. This may mean you are under- or overestimating your ability, or exaggerating the difficulty before you. It may mean you are reacting to past failures rather than memories of past succes-

[78]Ibid. 121-23.
[79]Ibid 205-06.
[80]Maltz, op. cit., 46.
[81]Ibid. 79.

ses. Knowing this, you are free to accept or reject those negative fear-feelings.[82]

4. Keep your goal in mind. The problem is not to control fear, but to control the choice of which tendency shall receive emotional reinforcement.[83]

5. Do not mistake excitement for fear. Until you direct the feeling of excitement or nerves (the effect of adrenalin), the feeling is nothing but pent-up emotional energy. It is a sign of additional strength to be used in any way you choose.

6. Crisis situations can be viewed either as opportunities or as tests. A change of attitude from "everything depends on this," to "I have everything to gain and nothing to lose" can help lessen the fear.[84]

7. Realize that your nervous system and your body cannot tell the difference between a real fear and an imagined one.[85]

Emery speaks of fear as a reaction to those past events which have turned out negatively. One way of conquering your fear is to RESPOND in life rather than react to it, so that you resolve it. Doing this will enable a person to express his emotions and feelings honestly instead of replaying all the negative images and thoughts that the mind brings up.[86] This different way of responding to a situation instead of reacting to it can help reduce fear.

In his book on stagefright, Robert Triplett cites two opposite kinds of fears; fear of failure and fear of success. Fear of failure is often predicated on past successes and these successes lead to greater perfectionism, more controls, and higher expectations. The critical voice in each of us embodies the desires for perfection and control, and we weaken because of its demands. Fear of success involves living up to higher standards as well as assuming greater responsibilities. Keeping things as they are is more comfortable, because the present

---

[82]Ibid. 236.
[83]Ibid. 217.
[84]Ibid. 222.
[85]Ibid. 224.
[86]Stewart Emery, *The Owner's Manual for Your Life* (New York: Pocket Books, 1982) 97.

condition is familiar, and familiarity means that one knows what to expect.[87]

Fear stimulates the sensations of weakness, contraction, and frigidity. There is a feeling of being exposed, vulnerable, and on the brink of danger. In the fear cycle, the stagefright emotion of fear looks toward its natural polarity: courage. Early on, an individual can choose to trust his preparation and accept whatever happens in the performance. In doing so the performer connects with the energy of courage. Without this courage, he seeks a mutated solution, desiring a kind of blind confidence, and the answer to fear is not found in this but rather in courage, courage to give in to the fear.[88] Below are some insights into performing through fear, given by Mr. Triplett.

> Accepting the fear silences the stagefright voices.
>
> A performer should trust in his preparation.
>
> Accept whatever happens and the voices will have nothing to talk about.
>
> If you try to fight or run away from fear, you feel a sense of panic.
>
> Give in to its energy by choice and you give up the fear of fear.
>
> Choose to perform without worry.
>
> Allow yourself to fail and you open up the possibility of success.
>
> Recognize your critic's perfectionism with such phrases as "should," "ought," "must," and "have to."
>
> Be willing to accept the level of your next performance.
>
> Do not confuse the feeling of excitement and attention with fear.
>
> Try to disidentify with the stagefright voices a half hour before a performance.
>
> Do not think in "I" messages, but talk to yourself in second-person ("you") or third-person ("he, she, or it").
>
> Contact your higher self and ask for guidance.[89]

---

[87]Triplett, op. cit., 49-51.
[88]Ibid. 61-62.
[89]Ibid. 180-82.

Regarding fear, Eloise Ristad, in her book, *A Soprano on Her Head*, suggests playing the ultra-observant detective and finding some solid information about how your body responds before and during a performance. Know what goes on inside your body. Do not try to control your symptoms and sensations, but rather, push them to the point where they can go no further. Try to increase the intensity and see how far you can carry any particular symptom. You may find that when you reach a certain point, the symptom actually reverses; that is to say, as soon as you try to intensify a symptom, it begins to disappear.

Ms. Ristad further states that if you are aware of your adrenalin flowing and do not try to suppress it, you can learn how to take it for granted and thus expect it.

> When you confront the symptoms head-on and demand that they increase in severity, you challenge your body and discover that it will produce only so much adrenalin, and when you find out exactly how much and what it will do to you, you lose some of the irrational fear of it.[90]

Allow yourself to be scared, and reinterpret those feelings as excitement. Fear and excitement come from the same adrenalin, so use the energy of adrenalin to live a little dangerously and channel it to give life to your performance. "Interpret those feelings as positive, stimulating, and energizing."[91]

The following excerpts are recommendations of Matthew McKay in his book, *Thoughts and Feelings*, on how to cope with fear.

> Fear is natural. It arises and subsides, and you can keep it under control.
>
> Worry won't make it any different.
>
> Just think rationally. Negative thoughts are not rational.
>
> You can plan how to deal with it.
>
> Take it one step at a time.
>
> Fear is a signal to relax.
>
> Take a deep breath, pause, and relax.

[90]Eloise Ristad, *A Soprano on Her Head* (Utah: Real People Press, 1982) 157-164.
[91]Ibid. 170.

It will soon be over, nothing lasts forever.

Worse things could happen.

Do something to take your mind off the fear.

Visualize a positive outcome.

Stay organized.

Keep your mind on the present, not on the past or future.

It's OK to make mistakes.

Being active will lessen the fear.

Picture someone you respect coping with this situation.[92]

TENSION AND PHYSICAL STRESS

In learning to deal with the pressures and anxiety of an audition, the resulting physical stress and its painful toll must not be overlooked. Some of the symptoms of tension include:

tense muscles (neck, back, arms, legs, etc)

dry mouth

increased heartbeat

sweaty hands

loss of breath

shaky fingers, arms, and knees

loss of ability to see or hear

stiff body movement

feeling sick

dizziness

trembling

palpitations

[92]Matthew McKay, Thoughts and Feelings (California: New Harbinger Publications, 1981) 52-53.

diarrhea

frequent urination

fatigue

giddiness

etc...

Tension is the performer's greatest obstacle, because it stifles the creative impulses and makes it impossible to express what one really feels. Before one does any work, performing or audition-ing, a person should try to relax and eliminate tension.[93]

Tension is elusive, moving from one part of the body to the other, sometimes very subtly. It is important to keep track of it and eliminate it, for the enemy of tension is exposure and if you allow the tension to stay hidden, it compounds itself.[94]

Although the symptoms and sensations of tension occur in an audition situation, the physical stress and the accompanying muscle tension block our awareness of the music and become the main concern of the moment. "All art is balance between tension and relaxation," says Ernst Toch, a composer and author. Hopefully, we can counterbalance the tension we feel with relaxation techniques to be explored in a later chapter.

The first thing that happens at a musical audition is that the performer must make an entrance either into the studio where the audition is taking place or onto the stage. Because of the discomfort and fear of auditioning the overall feeling is one of stiffness, coldness, and severity. It would be helpful to give ourselves some mental adjustment that will defuse this stiffness.[95]

The performer who is about to audition cannot resort to fight-or-flight. Stephen Aaron, in his book, *Stage Fright*, points out that the performer is physically and emotionally trapped. O. Fenichel, as quoted by Stephen Aaron, notes that panic anxiety sets in if a person has no opportunity to discharge the buildup of tension through a task,

---

[93]Eric Morris, *Being and Doing* (California: Spelling Publications, 1981) 18.
[94]Ibid. 25.
[95]Silver, op. cit., 1985) 106-07.

particularly 'if one is forced to wait quietly.' Flenichel also notes the sensation is one of 'feeling trapped.'"[96]

In his book, *Stage-Fright*, Robert Triplett speaks of tension and the stagefright response as being similiar to the fight-or-flight instinct. He says there is a dramatic shift of body energies that takes place to prepare for protective action, thus producing a variety of physical symptoms. The muscles throughout the body contract, preparing them to spring with a burst of energy (either to fight or to flee). In this contraction, the neck muscles pull the head down and the shoulders up, while the back muscles draw the spine into a concave curve. This in turn retracts the pelvis, pulling the genitals up in a vestigial protection reaction. In addition, the blood vessels constrict, the blood pressure elevates, and this heats up the entire mechanism. In an effort to cool the system down, perspiration is released, but since the blood is not flowing freely through the constricted vessels, especially the extremities, the sweat is cold. At the same time, the heart works extra hard to get blood to these areas. This is what causes the face to become flushed. The whole reaction gives us cold, clammy hands, and we feel hot under the collar.

The need for oxygen increases, as does our breathing rate, but with the diaphragm muscle shortened, our breaths are shallow and irregular. The interference with a person's normal breathing can range from hyperventilation to an unconscious holding of the breath.[97] Eyesight may also be distorted, because our pupils dilate to get a broader visual perspective, causing our vision to be unfocused. For this reason we sometimes lose our place when reading. To compound the entire problem, brain-wave frequency increases; this causes us to feel overwhelmed and confused, as if too much data were being "entered" into our heads. We feel as if things are happening too fast, and to compensate, the individual tends to speed up various processes such as speaking too fast, rushing tempos, and the like. Increased brain-wave activity changes the entire sense of timing and pacing, so that a variety of miscalculations are likely to surface. In surveying these various symptoms, we may conclude that one means of coping with the by-product of fear is by neutralizing its physical effects.[98] (See Chapter III, Relaxation techniques, p. 105.)

[96]Stephen Aaron, *Stage Fright* (Chicago: The University of Chicago Press, 1985) 81-82.
[97]Ibid. 83.
[98]Triplett, op. cit., 1983) 116-17.

Tension is felt before an audition in a three-phase development:

1. The momentary flashes of panic, manic agitation, moods of depression, and obsessional fantasies concerning the audition;

2. The stage manager's "15 minutes please!" when the performance becomes a psychic reality; and

3. The final phase where "a split between a functioning and an observing self" is felt. At the peak of anxiety "the observing self perceives the functioning self as off at a distance, operating mechanically before an audience which is also perceived at a distance."[99]

Sometimes there is a feeling of numbness that happens before a performance. This, in certain instances, can be considered as "the death of the creative spark within the actor" (performer). Performers accept stage fright as a part of their work to such an extent that they become worried when they feel "nothing" before a performance. Experience has taught them that, under such circumstances, their work will not be very good that night.

For some, anxiety and tension manifest themselves by causing a person to feel dizzy. Reasons for this may include:

1. respiratory aggravation resulting in hyperventilation and difficulty in breathing;

2. spatial disorientation due to the dilation of the pupils in the eyes; and

3. inner ear imbalance. The great actor/director Ingmar Bergman once noted that "rigor and dizziness are necessary for inspiration. . . . The dangerous routes are finally the only viable ones."[100]

Facing an impending audition can cause a great deal of tension. Perhaps the first step in overcoming and conquering the symptoms of physical stress is in recognizing you have them. In Chapter III there will be some answers to the questions of how to relieve the symptoms of tension.

---

[99]Aaron, loc. cit. 84.
[100]Ibid. 103.

EXPECTATIONS VERSUS CHALLENGES

When one takes an audition, the expectations one senses from others may exert heavy pressure. We feel we must live up to the demands of coaches, teachers, parents, or the judges. Blanketing the entire pressure picture is the whole issue of winning and losing. If we win, we are good; if we lose, we are bad, as if decreed by law.[101]

Psychologists have shown that the basic reason for a person's success is that he EXPECTED to succeed. Athletes who achieve success, for example, expect to win. Aristotle said, "What you expect, that you shall find." Expectations control your life, so it is imperative that you control your expectations. If you expect the best, the best you shall have. It then follows that expecting the worst to happen assures it will, and by permitting your life to be dominated by negative thought patterns you form the habit of expecting negative results. Most people have negative expectations at auditions.

Self-confidence can be built through POSITIVE EXPECTATIONS. You can build positive expectations by realizing that you have power within you to overcome any obstacle. So many people have a magnetic attraction to the past, as demonstated by their saving mementos, clippings, old letters, and trivia, and keeping scrapbooks. If you want to succeed, your mind must be geared to the future and perhaps these things should be replaced by pictures of what you want to accomplish; by visions of EXPECTATIONS of the great events which lie ahead.

When you find it necessary to reminisce, it thus makes sense to try to recapture some of the more pleasurable expectations you had as a child or young adult which have become reality. Take the time to consciously build on these and bring them up-to-date. Look forward to the future with expectation, then act enthusiastic.

Enthusiasm is a powerful force; the little-recognized secret of success. Derived from two Greek words, "en" meaning "in" and "theos" meaning "God," ENTHUSIASM means God in you. And it is this "God Power" within you which will enable you to accomplish anything you desire if you release it through dynamic thinking.[102]

---

[101]Triplett, op. cit., 3.
[102]Anthony, op. cit., 132-34.

If you notice you are paralyzed with fear about the consequences of your performance, you might experiment with reassessing your goals in order to find the meaning of your performance. Ask yourself what music means to you; what your experience goals are, and then what your performance goals are. When you have gotten "in touch" with your goals, go out there and play.[103]

Many of the feelings that accompany trying to live up to the standards of ourselves and the audition committee can be neutralized by "NOT GIVING YOUR WOULD-BE JUDGES OR JUDGES THAT POWER IN THE FIRST PLACE".[104] True, they may be in a position to give you a job, but that will happen only if they can use you. They may judge you to be a marvelous talent, but if you are not right for the position there is no earthly way you are going to get hired. The truth is that we are really never being judged in any situation outside of a court of law; all the judging is being done by ourselves. There is so much truth in the Biblical admonition, "judge not lest ye be judged." People who are self-judgmental are usually people who are highly critical of others. They do not accept themselves and they place great demands on themselves and on others. Unless they can temper this through therapy and/or a change in metaphysical outlook, they might be better off leaving the profession and becoming critics.[105]

In learning to deal with our judges, Eloise Ristad recommends the following, as taken directly from *A Soprano on Her Head*:

> Know the figures of authority and what they really want and need.
>
> Have a dialogue with them (in your imagination).
>
> Listen to what they expect you to be.
>
> Answer them clearly that you are only who you are.
>
> Ask them for support of whoever you happen to be.
>
> Ask them to pack all their expectations back into their traveling bag.
>
> Feel your goodness, your badness; your kindness, your meanness; your strength, your weakness; your talents, your un-

---

[103]Green, op. cit., 116.
[104]Silver, op. cit., 1985) 134.
[105]Ibid. 134.

talents; your dedication, your laziness. Feel all your opposites and their power. Without these opposites you would be bland and characterless. Feel how that power in your opposites reduces your judges to silly caricatures. Let those judges put on a show poking their fingers at you, jumping up and down with their silly demands, unrolling endless scrolls with their impossible list of exectations. Listen to them chatter and yammer at you. . . Turn your imagination loose with any image that joggles your funny bone, and when you have had enough, order them to leave, or zap them with judge dissolver. Look at your judges, now, with understanding. Love them a little as they are parts of you, and they really do mean well.

Flip to sensing the tyranny of your judges. Return to either your amused tolerance or to the strength in your honest anger. As we own our rage at our judges, we also own the energy that it takes to suppress that rage. When we have spent our rage at our judges, we free them to become non- judgmental guides.[106]

Relabeling our experience of being expected to produce a fine perormance can help relieve the stress felt. Our tendency is to label every experience we have, as for example "exciting" or "frightening" or "disappointing." The labels we choose determine the effect each experience will have on us. In other words, attaching labels like "crisis" over every experience, will give us an accumulated pile of troubles. On the other hand, if we use "challenge" labels, we will instead have OPPORTUNITIES. Also, labels can be changed according to what sort of stress results from a "bad" label. Donald Tubesing suggests that, instead of calling your life a can of worms, you should relabel it "non-vegetarian spaghetti."

Regarding the relabeling of stress provoking experiences, Tubesing recommends that you:

Rename your experience;

Choose the most positive label;

Put your troubles into a broader perspective (in 50 years from now who will know or care?);

[106]Ristad, op. cit., 13-16.

41

Use delays creatively (do something different with any free time);

Adopt the attitude of gratitude (be thankful for everything that happens to you).[107]

The resentment at having to produce at a given time and in a particular place is an important source of stagefright. Stephen Aaron suggests that some fantasies fearfully and angrily anticipate rejection of a repressed demand for love and approval at what is being produced. Performers want to be loved for what they produce, that is, for the gift they are giving. A portion of stagefright will vanish when you give yourself permission to screw up.[108]

When a performer is overwhelmed with the feeling of living up to the expectations of the audience or audition committee, he may feel he cannot measure up to the demands of the situation. The goal of changing this self-consciousness and of focusing back on the music being performed, is reached by FACING the fears we hold about the judges who are waiting to cast their vote as to our winning or losing. De-powering these figures of authority and going on to function with the necessary concentration is a way of breaking out of the ill-effects of the expectations the audition situation presents.

[107]Donald Tubesing, *Kicking Your Stress Habits* (Minnesota: Bolger Publications, 1981) 136.
[108]Aaron, op. cit., 101.

SELF-CONSCIOUSNESS

Performing without being self-conscious can help a person feel peaceful and assured. The fears of work-related problems can internally cause such self-doubt and insecurity that one's concentration can be broken and thus an audition ruined.

Having self-awareness and insight is a central ingredient to many theories of how to have a healthy personality and is a goal of a variety of current therapies. However, this tendency toward self-analysis and appraisal of one's thoughts and feelings signals psychological disturbance when it becomes obsessive. Being obsessively preoccupied with yourself is a sign that self- consciousness is a problem.[109]

Philip Zimbardo explains that self-consciousness has two dimen-sions: Public and Private.

PUBLIC SELF-CONSCIOUSNESS is reflected in a person's concern about his or her effect on others: ("what do they think of me?" "what kind of impression am I making?" "do they like me?" "how can I make sure they like me?"). If you are a publicly self-conscious type, you would respond with a "yes" to most of these following items:

I'm concerned about my style of doing things;

I'm concerned about the way I present myself;

I'm self-conscious about the way I look;

I usually worry about making a good impression;

I'm concerned about what other people think of me; and

I'm usually aware of my appearance.

PRIVATE SELF-CONSCIOUSNESS is the mind turned in on itself. It is not only the process of turning one's attention inward, but the negative content of that egocentric focus: ("I am inadequate" "I am inferior" "I am stupid" "I am ugly" "I am worthless"). Each thought is a candidate for investigation under a powerful analytical microscope. If you are a privately self-conscious person, you will answer yes to all or most of these items:

[109]Philip Zimbardo, *Shyness* (New York: Jove Books, 1977) 44.

> I'm always trying to figure myself out;
>
> Generally, I'm very aware of myself;
>
> I reflect about myself a lot;
>
> I'm often the subject of my own fantasies;
>
> I always scrutinize myself;
>
> I'm generally attentive to my inner feelings;
>
> I'm constantly examining my motives;
>
> I sometimes have the feeling that I'm off somewhere watching myself;
>
> I'm alert to changes in my mood; and
>
> I'm aware of the way my mind works when I work through a problem.[110]

The goal of self-searching, according to Freud, was to free persons from unreasonable barriers to action, and to help them be more in tune with both the tender and terrifying impulses. In contrast, to a self-conscious person, obsessive analysis becomes an end in itself, in that it stifles action by transferring the energy needed for the deed to the thought. The publicaly shy person is more concerned about BEHAVING badly, and the privately shy person is more concerned about FEELING badly.[111]

Understanding what makes us self-conscious can be classified in two groups: other people and situations. OTHER PEOPLE: Strangers, people of the opposite sex, authorities by virtue of their knowledge and their role, relatives, friends, and parents. SITUATIONS: When you are the focus of attention in a large group (as when giving a speech), social situations in general, new situations requiring assertiveness, when you are being evaluated, when you are the focus of attention in a small group, when you are vulnerable (needing help), and in small task-oriented groups.[112]

---

[110]Ibid., 45.
[111]Ibid., 46.
[112]Ibid., 54-55.

There are four basic kinds of change required when one begins to get rid of unwanted self-consciousness. They are, as quoted from Zimbardo's book, *Shyness*:

1. The way you think about yourself and about your self-consciousness;

2. The way you behave;

3. The relevant aspects of the way other people think and act; and

4. Certain social values that promote self- consciousness.

Here are his suggestions for helping a person break out of being self-conscious:

1. Recognize your strengths and weaknesses and set your goals accordingly.

2. Decide what you believe in.

3. Forgive yourself for mistakes, sins, failures, and past embarrassments. Give room to memories of past successes.

4. Look for the causes of your behavior in physical, social, economic and political aspects of your current situation and not in personality defects in you.

5. Remind yourself that there are alternative views to every event. "Reality" is never more than shared agreements among people to call it the same way rather than as each one separately sees it. This enables you to be more tolerant in your interpretation of other's intentions and more generous in dismissing what might appear to be rejections or put-downs of you.

6. Never say bad things about yourself: especially never attribute to yourself irreversible negative traits, like "stupid," "ugly," "a failure."

7. Don't allow others to criticize YOU as a person; it is your SPECIFIC ACTIONS that are open for evaluation and available for improvement. Accept such constructive feedback graciously if it helps you.[113]

[113]Ibid., 208-09.

8. Remember that sometimes failure and disappointment are blessings in disguise, telling you the goals were not right for you, the effort was not worth it, and a bigger letdown later on may be avoided.

9. Do not tolerate people, jobs, and situations that make you inadequate. If you can't change them or yourself enough to make you feel more worthwhile, walk on out, or pass them by. Life is too short to waste on downers.

10. Give yourself time to relax so you can get in touch with yourself.

11. Practice being a social animal. Enjoy feeling the energy that other people transmit, the unique qualities and range of variability of our brothers and sisters. Decide what you need from them and what they have to give. Then, let them know that you are ready and open to sharing.

12. Stop being over-protective about your ego; it is tougher and more resilient than you imagine. It bruises but never breaks.

13. Develop realistic long-range goals in life.

14. You are not an object to which bad things just happen. You are a unique individual who, as an active actor in life's drama, can make things happen. With confidence in yourself, obstacles turn into challenges and challenges into accomplishments. Self-consciousness then recedes, because instead of always preparing for and worrying about how you will live your life, you forget yourself as you become absorbed in the living of it.[114]

In applying this to performing and audition situations, we can say that self-consciousness is really "others- consciousness." In a performing situation we constantly receive feedback, good and bad, from a hundred different subtle clues. Clues of approval or disapproval, interest or lack of interest, continually advise us "how we are doing." Good performers can sense this constant communication and it helps them perform better. This communication from other people is used as negative feedback and good performers respond to it

---

[114]Ibid., 209-11.

automatically and creatively; more or less subconsciously and spontaneously, rather than consciously contrived or thought about.

When we become consciously concerned about what others think, too careful to consciously try to please other people, or too sensitive to the real or fancied disapproval of others, then we have excessive negative feedback, inhibition, and poor performance.[115]

Here are some suggestions by Maxwell Maltz:

1. Do not be concerned about the effect of your action.

2. Ignore excessive negative feedback.

3. Imagine being composed, relaxed, and doing all right and then act that way.

4. Concentrate on behaving, acting, and thinking as you do when you are alone, without any regard to how some other person might feel or judge you.

5. Practice performing first, before thinking, so you don't consider things too carefully.[116]

6. Don't plan or take thought about the audition before it starts. Act and correct your actions as you go along. Move first toward a goal and then correct any errors which may occur.

7. Stop criticizing yourself. Yearly self-appraisal is better than day-to-day critical feedback.[117]

8. Vividly picture yourself the way you want to be; act the part. Use your memory of a relaxed and spontaneous self.

9. Don't uncritically accept the ideas of others.

10. Don't REACT to a situation. Be an ACTOR. Within the context of your goal-striving structure, RESPOND and ACT in a manner which will further your progress.[118]

[115]Maltz, op. cit., 176-78.
[116]Ibid., 176-84.
[117]Ibid., 184-86.
[118]Ibid., 198.
[119]Ibid., 235.
[120]Branden, op. cit., 1977) 40-41.

11. Delay your self-consciousness for later. Stop scaring yourself to death with your own mental pictures.

12. Have faith and courage that the desired outcome is possible.[119]

In his book, *The Psychology of Self-Esteem*, Nathaniel Branden offers these suggestions to help self- consciousness:

1. The goal of awareness is set by giving oneself the order: "GRASP THIS." To letting the mind drift on its own accord is to be out of focus and we must then take command and find a goal for our attention.[120]

2. To be in focus is to know what one's mind is doing.

3. Letting the mind wander opens the inevitable consequences of non-thinking and the feelings of helplessness, of inefficacy, or anxiety, of the sense of living in an unknowable and inimical universe.[121]

4. Choose your goals and actions and be right in the choices you make. Realize that it is the conviction of your method of choosing that gives you your power of control over reality.[122]

As we become more self-conscious, there grows a need to protect ourselves as we feel increasingly more vulnerable. If we continue to protect ourselves, we heighten our self-consciousness but not our self-awareness. Real assurance is found in a seemingly strange way; that is, by giving up our protective measures and willfully entering into the block of our fear. If we enter this realm and accept whatever we may find, we can begin to move through the block of stagefright toward new qualities on the other side.[123]

There is a vulnerability that we feel when we realize that every new performance brings new opportunities for disaster or triumph. Barry Green suggests that unless we become vulnerable and accept the possibility of failure, we can never know how far our natural abilities can take us. When the performer risks an interpretation, the music really comes alive and to risk exposing yourself to the music

---

[121]Ibid., 46.
[122]Ibid., 199.
[123]Triplett, op. cit., 9.

means confronting the risk of failure.[124] For the audition taker, this means that you can cut through the self-conscious feelings of vulnerability by putting your attention totally on the music being performed.

Being in a situation that makes you self-conscious can dampen a performance, whether it be a concert or an audition. The ill effects of self-awareness can rob a person of confidence and this can lead to intense insecurity. This intense self- analysis and appraisal of one's thoughts can make one obsessively preoccupied with the self. The goal for keeping this self- conscious attention from turning in is that of finding new and creative means of turning the introspective attention outward.

[124]Green, op. cit., 124.

Chapter II

⟡⟡⟡

ON THE REALITIES OF THE MUSIC BUSINESS

LIFE IN THE ARTS

Unlike the business world, the amount of effort and time put in to master your craft in the arts does not pay off with predictable success. It is difficult to separate reality and fantasy when trying to be good enough to "make it." Because a musician is dependent on others to be hired for work, there is no surefire way to guarantee a steady income. Much of a musician's time is spent training with endless periods without work. During these times it is easy to develop a negative attitude with nagging questions such as, "What's it all for, anyway? I'm not working, so why break my back studying year after year?" Among the many reasons for the breakdown of belief, a major one is the lack of reward and recognition of society.

If you are willing to accept the realities of the field you have chosen, you will be far ahead of those who still live in fantasy. If you know the odds and face them honestly, it will be much easier to do what you must do. As musicians, we must find the joy and fulfillment of working on the craft an end in itself.[1] We become better musicians by realizing that we love to perform and the creative process thrills us.

Eric Morris says in his book, *Being and Doing*:

What makes you an artist is the fulfillment that comes from falling in love with the process. Naturally you want to work and earn a living at your art, and that is as it should be. If you are talented, if you develop that talent, if you commit yourself to a life of growth, and if you have the will and tenacity to stick in there, you will ultimately succeed. One of the greatest tragedies of history is that the artist Vincent Van Gogh sold only one painting in his life. But his love for his art and his

---

[1]Eric Morris, *Being and Doing* (California: Spelling Publications, 1981) 161.

51

passionate commitment to it must have given him something that most people don't even know exists.[2]

Morris presents the following ways to start learning to be responsible for your life as a musician:

1. Find a good teacher and focus on your training.

2. Practice every day.

3. Keep your peace of mind by fulfilling your financial responsibilities.

4. Take and use all productive criticism.

5. Work in the theatre whenever possible.

6. Find every opportunity to perform.

In learning to deal with inactivity and depression, the same writer recommends the following:

1. Understand the realities of the profession you have chosen.

2. Deal with money. Get a job and fulfill your financial obligations.

3. Exercise your body.

4. Diversify your creative energy: paint, write, and do activities that keep you productive and minimize depression.

5. Get with a supportive teacher.

6. Fill your life with active and productive people.

7. Keep a journal; write down your activities and thoughts so you can relate to them at another time.

8. Set goals for yourself that you can accomplish daily.

9. Involve yourself in a variety of stimulating activities.

10. Read! Read! Understand your field and the people who have made important discoveries and contributions.[3]

[2]Ibid. 161.
[3]Ibid. 164.

Because of the constant frustrations encountered at many levels of the music world, it is important to have a healthy ego. When things are going well you feel good about yourself. When you feel unproductive, useless, and without direction, it is better to acknowledge your depression than to ignore, for then you can do something about it. The first step is to find out how you feel about yourself, both generally and in a variety of situations. You must be totally honest about what you discover, as this will keep you from basing your sense of ego, well-being and value as a human being on your work alone. Each day, remind yourself that you have value and important qualities as an individual apart from being a musician. This knowledge will not depreciate your commitment or love for your art, but will rather allow you to put it into proper perspective.[4]

Try to maintain your personal integrity by allowing yourself to know who you are and what you want. Train yourself to be the best you can and come to terms with your worth. When you trust that you have value as a person and an artist, you will not be willing to accept low-grade jobs for money. It is advisable not to perform with a group or conductor that you do not respect, for then you risk giving up your own level of reality in the work process, or abandoning your creative contribution out of fear that you might be replaced. Each time your principles and integrity are compromised, you give up something that erodes your strength, individuality, and ability to respect yourself. We exist in a business where most people are "running scared." It is often difficult to maintain your values, but this is the way to develop your true talent and unique point of view.

There are many traps into which a musician may fall. One of the biggest relates to doing anything that is not really coming from what you feel. Try to become familiar with who you are and how you feel, and learn to express that moment-to-moment. Tension can also be a trap, as it suppresses your real emotional flow. If you acknowledge the presence of tension, it will lose its grip on you. Pressure is another trap as it represents "the moment of truth," so learn to take the time to relax and demand your due as an artist. In addition, try to use your time productively toward further training.

It seems as if being a musician at this time is similar to surviving as an artist in the 17th and 18th centuries. You were either in the employ of the

---

[4]Ibid. 172.

Aristocracy (the modern day equivalent of an orchestral position or having college tenure) or you had other means of making a living while performing occassionally (free-lancing or employment outside of music). Actors accept the fact that they work only 10% of the time and feel good about themselves working "secular" jobs. Today, when only 15% of college/conservatory students gain employment with an established orchestra, it is a good idea to have mastered a secondary skill you can bank on. The uncertainty of depending on others for basic survival is reason enough to take control over your money-making life.

If you have a craft and get into trouble, go to your craft and it will get you out of that trouble. Work for reality and creativity, and not approval. You know when what you are doing feels right, and you know when it doesn't. It is good to remember "THIS IS MY ONE AND ONLY LIFE. IF I AM NOT FOR ME, THEN WHO WILL BE?"[5]

DEALING WITH CRITICISM

In learning to function in the professional music world, a musician must learn to cope with criticism. Unlike self-criticism and negative self-talk, being criticized by conductors, colleagues, or the audition committees can devastate a performer's enthusiasm and confidence. Sometimes criticism at an audition at a critical time can be helpful, as it may improve the piece you are performing at the time. Other times, though, it may leave a deep wound if this type of feedback is not used productively.

A casual comment by a conductor (or committee) can trigger interference and negative reactions that may seriously inhibit the musicians he is supposedly leading. At times like these, it is helpful to perceive the criticism as an incorrect delivery of relevant material. When "right or wrong" criticism is given, it is seen as a command to "fix" it and "do" something differently. The "do this" attitude conveys a value judgment and does not give the performer the supportive awareness to convey that for which the conductor or committee is looking.[6]

Negative feedback is equivalent to criticism and says, in effect, "you are wrong," or "you are off course," or "you need to take corrective action to

---

[5]Ibid. 190.

[6]Barry Green, *The Inner Game of Music* (New York: Anchor Press, 1986) 197-99.

get back on course." The purpose of negative feedback, however, is to modify response and change the course of forward action; not to stop it altogether. If a person is too sensitive to negative feedback, he over-corrects and will perform in an exaggerated way; he may even stop all forward progress. We must have negative feedback in order to operate purposely, or to be guided to a goal.[7]

In coping with criticism, David Burns states three ways to react:

1. "I'M NO GOOD" RESPONSE
   THOUGHT: I'm worthless and I'm no good
   FEELING: Sad, anxious
   BEHAVIOR: Isolation, moping, giving up
   OUTCOME: Depression

2. "YOU'RE NO GOOD" RESPONSE
   THOUGHT: That stupid SOB is on my back again
   FEELING: Angry and frustrated
   BEHAVIOR: Obscenities and accusations
   OUTCOME: You fume for days, constantly telling yourself the world is no damn good.

3. SELF-ESTEEM RESPONSE
   THOUGHT: Here is a chance to learn something
   FEELING: Secure
   BEHAVIOR: You inquire for answers

OUTCOME: The problem is defined and a solution is proposed. You experience self-esteem and mood elevation.[8]

It would seem, then, that there are three ways to utilize the committee's criticism at an audition.

1. Respect their criticism and use it as a learning experience.
   A. Accept the fact that you are a creator and what you are creating is what you need to create. Likewise, respect that what

---

[7]Maxwell Maltz, *Psycho-Cybernetics* (New York: Prentice-Hall, Inc., 1980) 169-70.
[8]David D. Burns, M.D., *Feeling Good* (New York: William Morrow and Co., Inc., 1980) 132.

the committee is looking for will fulfill their needs and your style (whatever it may be), may not be what they want.[9]

B. Positive self-motivation begins with changing your awareness. To make a constructive change in your life, you must evaluate the potential benefits for any given action. Then you must convince yourself that the benefits will justify or outweigh the price you have to pay for them. Motivate yourself by profit and loss comparison.[10]

C. When someone is criticizing or attacking you, consider that his motive may be to help you. Be empathetic and agree with him so as to understand exactly what he means. Perhaps you can use the feedback for negotiation.[11]

2. Reject their criticism because you disagree with them and do not respect them.

A. Develop self-reliance by believing you can handle things that come up and heed your inner feelings for a hint of the kind of success you SHOULD want. Take your cue from what you are, not by listening to something outside yourself. Try to get an idea of what you want to become.[12]

B. Comparison can be seen as a sign of poor self-esteem. When you are compared with others you imagine yourself to be below everyone else. Avoid allowing your primary concern to be that of "one-upmanship," for this causes much of life to lose its enjoyment.[13]

C. Know that situations such as an audition are based on VALUE-JUDGMENTS such as, good and bad, right and wrong, fair and unfair. Value judgments are totally UNFOUNDED because inevitably you do what you have to, whether it is correct or incorrect. This is all your present awareness will allow; no more and no less.[14]

---

[9]Robert Anthony, *Total Self-Confidence* (San Diego: Berkley Publishing Corporation, 1979) 60.

[10]Ibid. 54.

[11]Burns, loc. cit. 123-28.

[12]Anthony, loc. cit. 16.

[13]Ibid. 24-25.

[14]Ibid. 50.

D. "It is OK to be angry at the audition committee. There is great strength in your honest anger."[15]

E. "Try to put the experience in perspective and make fun of the situation. Make cartoon caricatures of your judges and use your violent and playful fantasies to carry out all your hostilities and fears."[16]

3. Blame yourself and admit that you are no good.

A. This, of course, is unhealthy, but it is important to catch yourself saying this so that you can acknowledge this fear and get on with your life.

In learning to handle criticism, we must counteract its power by bringing up a very important part of us; the commender. The tranquil feelings that come from the commender bring about encouragement and enable us to notice our valuable aspects, in spite of our shortcomings. The unique contributions we each have to offer give us the "quiet" self-esteem for which we are looking. The perfectionist-critic discounts what we have, and commands that we pursue unattainable perfectionism. The commender listens to the critic in order to gain credence and both the critic and commender weigh our actions. Their evaluative abilities play off one other, finding fusion in compassion. It is from this compassion for ourselves that we get honest evaluations and a feeling of caring that is so valuable in learning to deal with criticism.[17]

DEALING WITH FAILURE

At an audition, a person either wins or loses. By the very nature of auditioning there can be only one person who fulfills the requirements of the audition committee. We need to come to terms with the realization that if 100 people show up to try out, 99 of them will be "losers."

No one wants to fail, but failure is something that everyone has to experience at sometime or another. We tend to become complacent about our successes, but we learn through our failures; a child learns to

[15]Eloise Ristad, *A Soprano on Her Head* (Utah: Real People Press, 1982) 16.
[16]Ibid. 21.
[17]Robert Triplett, *Stage-fright Letting It Work For You* (Chicago: Nelson-Hall, 1983) 91-92.

walk only by failing. Despite what you may believe, there is an infinite number of second chances. Also, if we look back on all of our past losses, we realize that memories are short, and failures are not remembered for long in this business. If we look at an audition as a "learning process," then the fear of failure would not have that much power. To help rob this fear of its power it may help to regularly audition for jobs you do not really want. This lessens the audition's importance and makes it a great deal easier to audition for jobs you do want.[18]

A person who is afraid of failing may have grown up with the expectation that he will be special, perfect, or extraordinary, and believes that his performance is living proof of his worth. As one tests himself in the world he encounters failure. However, since these people are afraid that one failure will prove they are worthless, they are unable to do their best and so hold back a little to save face. Ironically, the little they hold back is just what they need to succeed.

Of course, almost everyone fears failure and any great test of his worth. School exams and the dread they cause are good examples of this. Few people ever reach one hundred percent of their capacity because of a certain amount of fear in trying. You cannot do your best unless you like yourself and are willing to accept your own realistic limitations. Even if your best work is rejected, you should still be able to feel good about being you. Unfortunately, this is not always easy to remember, especially when you are having an off day or week.[19]

Many people whose lives are one continual failure after another are really punishing themselves as a way of getting even with others. They feel guilty about being angry at someone for not loving them. It seems a circuitous and fruitless route to take in comparison with accepting reality and moving on. A risk of esteem is not a failure if it offers you a chance to test your ideas about yourself, to push yourself, to try your talents and see what you are worth, and to grow to the next step. Each person determines what he makes of his experience, but you cannot find yourself unless you risk failing.

There is nothing as difficult as putting your best on the line, except perhaps to yearn for successes that will never happen because you are too afraid to risk. A risk of esteem is successful when you do your best and

[18]Fred Silver, *Auditioning for the Musical Theatre* (New York: Newmarket Press, 1985) 137-38.

[19]David Viscott, *Risking* (New York: Simon and Schuster, Inc., 1977) 128.

accept your performance as an honest reflection of yourself. There will always be some part of your performance that is not perfect no matter how extensive your preparations. A successful risk of esteem makes you more willing to risk the next time because you have overcome your hesitation to be yourself.[20]

It is important not to judge yourself on the outcome alone regardless of your individual effort. How you interact at an audition is the process over which you have control, while how the committee reacts is the product in which you have no say. Remember that you can pride yourself on good, consistent work regardless of the outcome of any particular audition.[21]

Here are some guidelines to follow to help deal with failure:

1. MAKE FRIENDS WITH FAILURE. Failure is a necessary part of growth. There is nothing wrong in failing.

2. DO NOT BE CONCERNED WITH WHAT OTHERS THINK. Your need for approval makes you want to look good in front of friends, family and society.

3. DO NOT COMPARE YOURSELF TO OTHERS. Someone else will always have assets you do not have.

4. GIVE UP YOUR NEED FOR APPROVAL. It will not matter how many mistakes you make.

5. MAKE PERSISTENCE YOUR GOAL. This quality separates the achievers from the non-achievers.[22]

6. DO NOT GIVE YOUR DOMINANT THOUGHTS TO FAILURE. Failure is rehearsed by constant repetition.

7. HAVE A POSITIVE MENTAL PICTURE. Have a positive belief in yourself.

8. BE WILLING TO FACE FAILURE. Accept the worst that can happen and you will be prepared for it. Then you will be able to meet and successfully handle other challenges.

---

[20]Ibid, 200-01.
[21]Burns, loc. cit., 84.
[22]Anthony, loc. cit., 131-32.

9. WORRY MEANS YOU ARE NOT IN THE PRESENT TIME ZONE. If you are living in the present it is impossible to worry.

10. HAVE A SENSE OF HUMOR. Humor is a safety valve to keep yourself from taking yourself too seriously.

11. KEEP IN MIND THE PLEASURE YOU RECEIVE. The benefits of your talents and insights give meaning to yourself and others.[23]

12. FROM EVERY FAILURE THERE IS A LESSON TO BE LEARNED. It increases your capacity to meet new problems.[24]

13. FAILING DOES NOT MAKE YOU A ROTTEN PERSON. It is unfortunate that you failed, but you will not always fail.

14. YOUR VALUE IS NOT PROPORTIONAL TO YOUR ACCOMPLISHMENTS. No one can display perfect adequency and achievement.

15. ACHIEVEMENT DOES NOT RELATE YOUR INTRINSIC WORTH. You do not change your worth by your successes.[25]

16. ALLOW YOURSELF TO FAIL. Allowing yourself to fail opens up the possibility of allowing yourself to succeed.[26]

17. TRUST IN YOUR NATURAL TALENTS. Trying to remain in control makes you feel embarrassed or insulted and feeds the fear of failure.[27]

18. YOU ARE OKAY EVEN WHEN YOU MAKE MISTAKES. Being human allows us to make mistakes part of the time.

19. FAILING IS MERELY LEARNING. Tune in to the information available in all of your experiences and try not to attach labels of good/bad or success/failure to experiences.

20. GET INFORMATION AND FEEDBACK. Use failure to get facts for use on future successes.[28]

[23]Ibid. 168-73.

[24]Harry Lorayne, *Secrets of Mind Power* (New York: Signet, 1975) 79.

[25]Albert Ellis, *A New Guide to Rational Living* (New Jersey: Prentice-Hall, Inc., 1975) 102-04.

[26]Triplett, loc. cit., 176.

[27]Green, loc. cit. 107.

[28]Ristad, loc. cit., 143-44.

In learning to deal with failures at auditions it is helpful to have new ways to interpret a defeat. Distorted thinking oftentimes will make us yield to an emotional "I give up" type of surrender. The self-doubts and depression that arise from a lost audition can be turned around if we learn to use the information we have gathered from the experience or if we reject the judgment passed down from those figures of authority whom we do not respect.

OVERCOMING JEALOUSY

One of the realities of the music business is that other people may do things better than you. How much time do we spend being envious, jealous, bitter, and angry? Many performers complain about the industry and put down other performers and their success. When we enter the warm-up room to prepare to play our audition, we hear our competition performing those passages about which we feel insecure, faster, louder and in a word, perfectly. The emotions which arise when we feel threatened are hard to cope with, but they must be approached in the most healthy way or they will distract us for the duration of the audition, and even for the rest of our lives.

In her book, *A New Look At Love*, Elaine Walster describes jealousy as having two basic components:

1. a feeling of battered pride, and

2. a feeling that one's property rights have been violated.

Margaret Mead observes that the more shaky one's self-esteem, the more vulnerable one is to jealousy. Jealousy records the degree of insecurity. It is a negative, miserable state of feeling, having its origin in the sense of insecurity and inferiority.

Sociologist Kingsley Davis provides a fascinating analysis of jealousy:

"There are thus two dangers which beset any person with regard to property. The first is that somebody will win out over him in legitimate competition. This is the danger of superior rivalry. The second is that somebody will illegitimately take from him property already acquired. . . . This is the danger of trespass. . . . Most malignant emotions are concerned with these two dangers, being directed either at a rival or trespasser or at someone who is helping a rival or trespasser. . . . In general fear and hatred of rivals is institutionally suppressed; fear and hatred of trespassers encouraged. . . . Our malignant emotions, fear, anger, hate, and jealousy, greet any illicit attempt to gain property that we hold."[29]

CONTROLLING JEALOUSY

Elaine Walster recommends the following steps to control jealous feelings:

1. TRY TO FIND OUT EXACTLY WHAT IT IS THAT IS MAKING YOU JEALOUS. Usually, you can pinpoint something specific about the situation which is bothering you. Two key questions to ask are:

   What was going on in the few moments before you started to feel this way? and,

   What are you afraid of?

   Family therapist Larry Constantine lists several situations that often trigger jealousy:

   Feeling that you're no longer "number one". . . and everyone knows it.

   Feeling upset because you can't predict what's going to happen. Feeling powerless. Realizing you can't control your life. Feeling emotionally or intellectually deprived. Thus, the first step is to try to understand WHAT you feel and WHY you feel this way.

2. TRY TO PUT YOUR JEALOUS FEELINGS IN PERSPECTIVE. Be in touch with what is a rational component and what is an irrational one. We should, and can, abandon our irrational

[29]Elaine Walster, *A New Look at Love* (Massachusetts: Addison-Wesley Publishing Co., 1978) 87-88.

ideas. Force yourself to consider each jealously-arousing situation more realistically. You can gain even more control if you can manage to change the situation.

3. NEGOTIATING A "CONTRACT." Once you know exactly what makes you jealous, you can begin to negotiate; that is, bargain with yourself to find a balance in hopes of becoming more comfortable with the situation.[30]

In his book, *Being and Doing*, Eric Morris suggests these valuable ideas to help us overcome envy:

Try imagining that each of us is climbing our own mountain and that each mountain has its unique obstacles. If you can think about your journey as being unlike anyone else's, you will stop comparing yourself to others.

Make a list of all your daily activities and pick out those that cause you to waste time feeling envious of others and replace them with more productive involvement.

The next time you notice that you are putting someone down or feeling bitter about your place in life, ask yourself just what you are accomplishing. In this country it is possible to have anything for which you dream as long as you figure out how to get it.

Concerning ourselves with what other people have should only serve the purpose of showing us that it is possible for us to get what we want.[31]

SEPARATING OUR SELVES FROM OUR WORK

As has been stated previously, it is very difficult for any artist not to identify his worth by how well he does in his profession. A performer spends years working to achieve some excellence so as to feel good about himself, as well as to gain acceptance and affection. Problems occur when we do not achieve success, and the frustrations that go along with a career in the arts only add to the problem. Again, underlying the entire situation is the whole issue of winning and losing.

[30]Ibid. 90-93.
[31]Morris, Loc. cit., 181.

The pages in this section will be devoted in large part to direct quotes only. This is intended so that the reader can examine word-for-word some valuable material compiled from several sources, on this important topic of self-worth as a human being.

Robert Anthony writes:

> In seeking recognition and praise, a person can easily become addicted to approval. Praise-seeking implies that you must constantly prove your worth. Every time you make a mistake or do something you feel does not meet someone else's standards, you feel less than others. You then blame yourself and feel guilty for not doing what you think you should. You keep on asking yourself, "Have I done well enough?" But the person who goes through life trying to do "well enough" develops the compulsive need to be or do "better than" others. And so one ill is piled on top of another. No matter how hard you try to be better than someone in any given area, you will feel inadequate because there are always those who, in your eyes, have surpassed you. They will have more money, larger homes, greater prestige, better physical attributes, etc. It is a game you can never win. . . . The most destructive power of praise lies in its ability to make you identify with your actions. Praise says, in effect, that you are "good" because of your "good" acts and "bad" if you make a mistake or act 'badly.' . . . . If you are to be totally free and self-confident, you must cease being caught in the trap of praise-seeking. To break this destructive habit, you must stop PLACING OTHERS ABOVE YOURSELF. Never look up to anyone for any reason. If you do this you will never have to seek their approval and will no longer be seduced by praise or intimidated by blame.[32]

You may consider yourself good, almost good, talented, or untalented. None of these really describes you. They are only descriptions of the things you do or the actions you take. If you identify solely with your actions, you are falsely perceiving the truth about yourself. You are judging, limiting, and even rejecting yourself without justification.

---

[32]Anthony, loc. cit., 27-28.

YOU ARE NOT YOUR ACTIONS. Your actions are only the MEANS you use to fulfill your dominant needs. They may be WISE or UNWISE but this does not classify you as "good" or "bad." At the very source of your being, you are a perfect individual who, for the moment, may be acting upon a faulty Awareness. . . then. . . you must already be perfect but are prevented from this realization by your existing Awareness.[33]

In trying to understand the relationship of man to his work, Nathaniel Branden contends that it is important to distinguish between pride and self-esteem.

Pride pertains to the pleasure a man takes in himself on the basis of and in response to SPECIFIC achievements or actions. Self-esteem is confidence is one's capacity to achieve values. Pride is the consequence of having achieved some particular value(s). Self-esteem is "I can." Pride is "I have." The deepest pride a man can experience is that which results from his achievement of self-esteem: since self-esteem is a value that has to be earned, the man who does so feels proud of his attainment.

If, in spite of his best efforts, a man fails in a particular undertaking, he does not experience the same emotion of pride that he would feel if he had succeeded; but, if he is rational, HIS SELF-ESTEEM IS UNAFFECTED AND UNIMPAIRED. His self-esteem is not, or should not be, dependent on PARTICULAR successes or failures, since these are not necessarily in a man's direct, volitional control and/or not in his exclusive control. The failure to understand this principle causes an incalculable amount of unnecessary anguish and self-doubt. If a man judges himself by criteria that entail factors outside his volitional control, the result, unavoidably, is a precarious self-esteem that is in chronic jeopardy.[34]

The author of *A New Guide to Rational Living* has written:

Technically, you "are" not any particular thing. David Bourland, Jr., a student of general semantics, points out that whenever you use any form or the verb "to be," you speak incorrectly. You "are" not a butcher, baker, or candlestick maker. You "are" only, if anything, a

---

[33]Ibid. 73-74.
[34]Nathaniel Branden, *The Psychology of Self-Esteem* (New York: Bantam Books, 1981) 125-26.

human individual who PRACTICES these various kinds of occupations, but who also practices many other things. . . . To identify, much less to rate your SELF according to your performance of some particular human activity, tends to create the illusion that you, a person, have only as much worth as that activity. And how much sense does that make?[35]

David D. Burns, M.D. shares the following:

A silent assumption that leads to anxiety and depression is "My worth as a human being is proportional to what I have achieved in my life." This attitude is at the core of Western culture and the Protestant work ethic. It sounds innocent enough. In fact, it is self-defeating, grossly inaccurate, and malignant. People are especially vulnerable to concerns about career failure because they've been programmed from childhood to base their worth on their accomplishments.

What are the disadvantages of the philosophy, "worth equals achievement"? First, if your business or career is going well, you may become so preoccupied with it that you may inadvertently cut yourself off from other potential sources of satisfaction and enjoyment as you slave away from early morning to late night. As you become more and more of a workaholic, you will feel excessively driven to produce because if you fail to keep up the pace, you will experience a severe withdrawal characterized by inner emptiness and despair. In the absence of achievement, you'll feel worthless and bored because you'll have no other basis for self-respect and fulfillment.[36]

Dr. Burns recommends four paths to attain self-esteem if your worth does not come from your success or from love or approval:

1. ACKNOWLEDGE THAT HUMAN "WORTH" IS JUST AN ABSTRACTION THAT DOES NOT EXIST. . . .There is actually no such thing as human worth. Therefore, you cannot have it or fail to have it, and it cannot be measured. Worth is not a "thing," it is just a global concept. It is so generalized it has no concrete practical meaning. . . . It is simply self-defeating. . . so rid yourself IMMEDIATELY of ANY claim to being "worthy," and

---

[35]Ellis, loc. cit., 102-04.
[36]Burns, loc. cit., 289.

you'll NEVER HAVE TO MEASURE UP again or fear being "worthless."

2. RATHER THAN GRASPING FOR "WORTH," AIM FOR SATISFACTION, PLEASURE, LEARNING, MASTERY, PERSONAL GROWTH AND COMMUNICATIONS WITH OTHERS. . . . Acknowledge that everyone has one "unit of worth" from the time they are born until the time they die. . . . During your lifetime, you can enhance your happiness and satisfaction through productive living, or you can act in a destructive manner and make yourself miserable. But your "unit of worth" is always there, along with your potential for self-esteem and joy.

3. RECOGNIZE THAT THERE IS ONLY ONE WAY YOU CAN LOSE A SENSE OF SELF-WORTH BY PERSECUTING YOURSELF WITH UNREASONABLE, ILLOGICAL, NEGATIVE THOUGHTS. Self-esteem can be defined as the state that exists when you are not arbitrarily haranguing and abusing yourself but when you choose to FIGHT BACK against those automatic thoughts with meaningful, rational responses.

4. SELF-ESTEEM CAN BE VIEWED AS YOUR DECISION TO TREAT YOURSELF LIKE A BELOVED FRIEND. Don't peck away at your weaknesses and imperfections. Treat yourself as a VIP and then self-torment will look pretty silly.[37]

The role of the performer in society is not like some other professions which provide the basic material necessities of life. The pursuits of an artist contribute immeasurably to the quality of life; their tasks carry a certain hint of illusion; they are one step removed from everyday existence. Each profession has its persona; a stereotypical role-model a performer plays out, as if playing out a script. These stereotyped roles are adapted as a way to protect our private self from vulnerability. This vulnerability stems from a fear that a public performance threatens our life. An imagined fear of physical danger is actually a fear that our sense of identity is being threatened. Our self-esteem and pride feel as if they are on the line and this feeling stimulates our protection response. Because we want

---

[37]Ibid. 299-302.

to be civilized and to be a "nice person," we remain composed and adopt this specific role identification.

Robert Triplett says that these restrictive identifications are precisely the ones that produce the feelings of vulnerability we would like to avoid.

> If, however, we identify ourselves with much broader archetypal concepts such as being a man or woman, a learner, or a child of the universe, the daily fluctuations of adversity pale to insignificance. We do not feel vulnerable because we are a man, woman, or even an American. We feel so because we identify ourselves with a more specific idea which for one reason or other is important to us: "I am a great musician."
>
> Narrow role identifications such as this one distort our self-concept, since as human beings we are composed of much more than they imply. Furthermore, in maintaining such a narrow sense of identity, our self-concept is tested with each performance, and the more important the event, (such as an audition), the more likely it is that this identification will face devastation. If a performance or an audition does not meet our expectations, we begin to feel that we are not worthy. Also, specific role identifications make us feel isolated as if to say its "me against them" and, consequently, to feel increased vulnerability.[38]

Without being acutely aware of our roles and how often and well we "play" them, extremely narrow role identification can turn into the exact opposite of what we want. Just because a performer has reached the peak of success, it does not mean that new fears of failure will not crop up with each new achievement. We may be an audience favorite, but as our stardom rises we become more frightened.[39]

Maxwell Maltz states that:

> This seeking for identity, the desire for selfhood, the urge to be "somebody" is universal, but we make a mistake when we seek it in conformity, in the approval of other people, or in material things. It is a gift of God. You ARE ; period. Admit to yourself that you may not be perfect and that you may have faults and weaknesses. Say to

---

[38]Triplett, loc. cit., 3-6.
[39]Ibid. 6.

yourself, "I may have a long way to go, but I AM SOMETHING and I will make the most of that something."[40]

It is important to be able to separate our self from our performance. No matter what the outcome of an audition or a performance, it is necessary to be able to say to yourself, "I'm OK, so what if my performance was good or bad." If you can give yourself the privilege of being whatever you happen to be at that moment, without condemning yourself ahead of time, you are free enough to allow a flop, and as it turns out you are usually free enough not to have one.[41]

"In the realm of his work, the primary desire of a man of self confidence is to face challenges, to achieve and to grow; the primary desire of the man lacking in self-confidence is to be 'safe.'" Learning to separate ourselves from our work can help us find this self-confidence.[42]

[40]Maltz, loc. cit., 126.
[41]Ristad, loc. cit., 173-74.
[42]Branden, loc. cit. 131. 73-74.

Chapter III

―❦❦―

COPING STRATEGIES AND TECHNIQUES

FINDING CONTROL UNDER PRESSURE

The next two chapters are designed to help the auditioner cope with the pressures and tensions of auditioning. The techniques that are being offered are to be used at the actual event to help maintain focus and efficiency. Preparing mentally before a performance is important to cultivate a calm body, an anxiety-free mind, and an understanding of how the body reacts to the signals of adrenalin.

The many feelings and emotions that are experienced at an audition have to be understood and accepted. If a person takes these feelings as a "solid truth" and believes that what they are saying should actually be considered, the person is paralyzed with confusion and fear. Learning to accept the feelings of the moment as a measure of what you like and dislike can guard against being overwhelmed by self-destructive thoughts.

A person's inner dialogue during an audition can be helpful or disabling. The self-talk and "chatter" that occurs can be controlled or ignored depending upon the discipline of each individual person. Learning not to be distracted by the thoughts that pop up can be of great help to a person in a performance.

Concentration is sometimes interfered with during times of stress. A performer's attention can easily be distracted and unwanted mistakes can creep in. Learning to stay in focus and keep your attention concentrated during times of stress can be of great importance to a person undertaking an audition.

Much of the stress felt at an audition is manifested in tight muscles and bodily imbalance. A person can function with greater efficiency if the body is taught to relax and stay in alignment.

Using humor to counteract the stress and bad atmosphere of the audition environment can be a practical tool. Dispelling the negative thoughts and pressures by joking about it, either in a harmless or violent way, can change the way you feel about something that is bothering you.

A person's diet before an audition can affect the body in many ways. Making sure that not too much sugar is consumed before a performance will keep the body from feeling that "jittery" sensation which is sometimes confused with nerves. Drinking too much caffeine can also aggravate the nervous system while using natural relaxants, such as Dolomite and chamomile tea, can help a person to relax. Sometimes drugs can be abused with disastrous consequences, yet specific types can be of great help to a person who suffers from severe nerves or anxiety attacks.

Many strategies can therefore be used to help a person have a successful audition. A person can help hinself feel in control of a situation which could potentially be ridden with helplessness by learning what to say to himself, what to eat beforehand, and how to keep the body in a relaxed state.

PREPARING FOR AUDITIONING

Preparation for an audition entails mobilizing yourself on many levels. Besides the hours of preparing the materials, your instrument, your finances, and your health, there is also the priming of your emotional state. This section will introduce various methods of building an emotional foundation in anticipation of the stresses felt at an audition and will help the individual enjoy the experience more.

One of the most obvious problems we run across in preparing for an audition is having to deal with the automatic thoughts that pop up in our minds. When this occurs, it is important to counter them with a "ration"–a pre-prepared rational response. For example:

> AUTOMATIC THOUGHT: "If I'm not 'the greatest,' it means I won't get any attention from people."

RATIONAL RESPONSE: (all or nothing thinking) "Whether or not I'm 'the greatest,' people will listen to me, they will see me perform, and many will respond positively to my music."

AUTOMATIC THOUGHT: "But not everyone likes the music I play."

RATIONAL RESPONSE: "This is true of all musicians; no musician can please everyone. Quite a few people respond to my music. If I enjoy my music, then that should be enough."

AUTOMATIC THOUGHT: "But how can I enjoy my music if I know I'm not 'the greatest'?"

RATIONAL RESPONSE: "I'm playing music that turns me on, just as I always have. Besides, there is no such thing as 'the world's greatest musician.' So stop trying to be it!"

AUTOMATIC THOUGHT: "But if I were more famous and talented, then I'd have more fans. How can I be happy on the sidelines when the big-name performers with charisma are in the spotlight?"

RATIONAL RESPONSE: "How many fans and how much success do I need before I'll be happy?"

AUTOMATIC THOUGHT: "But I feel that no one could really love me until I become a big-name talent."

RATIONAL RESPONSE: "Other people are loved who are just 'average' in their work. Do I really have to be a big-shot before someone will love me?"[1]

When the mind is under stress while preparing an audition, it is difficult for it to think in a calm, logical, and controlled fashion. Usually thoughts come in short phrases, such as, "I'm not doing well," or "What am I doing here?" Because of this phenomenon, it is good to have a reserve of positive or helpful phrases to consciously inject into your thoughts. These short phrases will help ease the stress and anxiety felt days, hours, and seconds before an audition.

[1]David Burns, *Feeling Good* (New York: William Morrow and Co., Inc., 1980) 306.

In understanding and trying to control your thoughts and feelings, dividing the problems that arise into three categories will make it easier to put your sensations and internal messages into perspective. These categories are: 1) Thoughts (to give you focus and strength); 2) Fear (to help control and lessen its power), and 3) Adrenalin (to calm its physical effects on your body). The following four pages are devoted to some general comments, observations and suggestions on how to deal with each of the three potential problems directly before a performance.

THOUGHTS

THOUGHTS ARE NOT REAL, SO DON'T REACT TO THEM.

CONTEMPLATION PARALYZES THE SELF.

INTEND TO DO WELL AND ACCEPT WHAT HAPPENS.

JUDGMENT AND CRITICISM ARE NO-WIN GAMES.

CURIOSITY, UNDERSTANDING AND HUMOR ARE WINNING GAMES.

DON'T CARE WHAT PEOPLE THINK.

KEEP YOUR ATTENTION OUTWARD.

TALK BACK TO IRRATIONAL FEARS: SO WHAT IF.

WHATEVER HAPPENS, YOU'RE OK.

DON'T RATE YOUR PERFORMANCE.

WORRY AND PERFORMING DON'T GO TOGETHER.

ELIMINATE "HOW AM I DOING?" FROM YOUR VOCABULARY.

ATTENTION ON YOURSELF IS NOT NECESSARY.

WE ARE NEEDED IN THE WORLD.

IT'S OK TO MAKE MISTAKES.

ASSUME THE COMMITTEE LIKES YOU.

FLOAT, DON'T FIGHT.

CONCENTRATION MEANS BEING INTERESTED.

SEE THE GOOD IN THINGS.

LET GO OF JUDGES AND THEIR CRITICISM.

TURN OFF YOUR MONITORING SELF WHEN PERFORMING.

DON'T TALK TO YOURSELF, KEEP YOUR ATTENTION ON THE FLOW OF THE MOMENT AND TRUST YOURSELF.

TRUST YOUR INTENTION.

VIEW AUDITIONS AS A CHALLENGE, RATHER THAN AS FULFILLMENT OF AN EXPECTATION.

STRIVE FOR EXCELLENCE, NOT PERFECTION.

DON'T OBSESS ON THE EFFECTS OF ADRENALIN.

WHEN CONFUSED, THINK IN SHORT PHRASES, NOT SENTENCES.

REALIZE THIS SITUATION WILL PASS.

BE SPECIFIC ABOUT WHAT YOU FEAR, DON'T GENERALIZE.

TAKE SLOW AND DEEP BREATHS EVERY FOUR SECONDS.

KEEP YOUR THOUGHTS IN THE PRESENT, NOT THE FUTURE OR PAST.

NOTICE WHAT YOU ARE SAYING TO YOURSELF, IS IT HELPFUL?

BE GOOD TO YOURSELF, DON'T NEEDLESSLY TORTURE YOURSELF.

PUT OFF WORRY UNTIL IT WILL DO YOU SOME GOOD.

YOU CAN'T KNOW THE END RESULT NOW, SO GIVE UP THINKING ABOUT IT.

CONCENTRATE ON THE MUSIC.

ALLOW YOURSELF TO REACT NATURALLY TO YOUR THOUGHTS, THEN MANAGE THEM.

SUSPEND YOUR JUDGEMENT ON YOUR THOUGHTS AND FEELINGS.

NO THOUGHT OR FEELING IS RIGHT OR WRONG, JUST TRY TO RECOGNIZE THEM.

NEGATIVE THOUGHTS WILL GO AWAY IF YOU DON'T PARTICIPATE IN THEM.

DON'T FANTASIZE ABOUT THE NEGATIVE CONSEQUENCES.

IT DOESN'T MATTER WHY THOUGHTS POP INTO YOUR CONSCIOUSNESS.

DON'T BRING UP BAD PAST EXPERIENCES.

VISUALIZE POSITIVE OUTCOMES.

ACCEPTANCE OF FEAR CAN DECREASE THE INTENSITY OF YOUR RESISTANCE TO IT.

DON'T CARE SO MUCH ABOUT WHAT WILL HAPPEN.

EXPECT WHAT'S EXPECTABLE.

DON'T CREATE A PHOBIC SPIRAL OF PANIC-ORIENTED SELF-STATEMENTS.

DON'T TEST HOW NERVOUS YOU CAN MAKE YOURSELF.

FIND THE JOY.

BY PREDICTING WHAT WILL HAPPEN, YOU WILL FEEL MORE IN CONTROL.

WHAT CAN YOU DO TO MAKE THIS SITUATION BETTER?

INVENT OPTIONS BY CREATING VARIATIONS!

HOW DO YOU WANT TO FEEL? CREATE YOUR OWN COMFORT.

BE HUMOROUS.

MAKE A HABIT OF INSERTING NEW, GOOD AND HEALTHY THOUGHTS

SAVE PHILOSOPHIZING FOR AFTER A PERFORMANCE OR AUDITION.

ENJOY LISTENING TO YOURSELF.

FEAR

DON'T OBSESS ON THE EFFECTS OF ADRENALIN.

LABEL AND NOTICE THE LEVEL OF YOUR ANXIETY (1-10).

IT'S OK TO BE NERVOUS.

BE SPECIFIC WITH WHAT YOU FEAR, NOT GENERAL.

TAKE SLOW AND DEEP BREATHS EVERY FOUR SECONDS.

CONCENTRATE ON THE MUSIC AND WHAT YOU'RE DOING.

ALLOW YOURSELF TO REACT NATURALLY TO FEAR, THEN MANAGE IT.

SUSPEND YOUR JUDGMENT ON YOUR THOUGHTS AND FEELINGS.

ACCEPTANCE OF FEAR CAN DECREASE THE INTENSITY OF YOUR REACTION TO IT.

IT'S NOT WORTH FIGHTING THE SYMPTOMS.

HOW DO YOU WANT TO FEEL? CREATE YOUR OWN COMFORT.

COUNT BACKWARDS TO RELAX (10 TO 1).

TURN OFF SENSORING WHEN PERFORMING.

FLOAT PAST THE FEAR, DON'T FIGHT IT.

IT'S OK TO MAKE MISTAKES.

WHATEVER HAPPENS, YOU'RE OK.

THOUGHTS ARE NOT REAL, SO DON'T REACT TO THEM.

ADRENALIN

DON'T BE SURPRISED THAT YOUR ADRENALIN IS FLOWING.

ADRENALIN GIVES STRENGTH AND POWER TO PERFORMANCES.

DON'T OBSESS ON THE EFFECTS OF ADRENALIN.

DON'T LET YOUR SENSATIONS OVERWHELM YOU, CO-EXIST WITH THEM.

EXPECT SOME SENSATIONS.

IT'S OK TO FEEL NERVOUS.

NOTICE AND LABEL THE LEVEL OF YOUR ANXIETY (1-10).

YOU CAN FUNCTION WHILE HAVING FEELINGS AND SENSATIONS.

TAKE SLOW AND DEEP BREATHS EVERY FOUR SECONDS.

ECONOMIZE YOUR ENERGY.

ALLOW YOURSELF TO REACT NATURALLY TO FEAR, THEN MANAGE IT.

NO THOUGHT OR FEELING IS WRONG – JUST RECOGNIZE THEM.

ALLOW FEELINGS TO ARISE.

ACCEPTANCE OF FEAR CAN DECREASE THE INTENSITY OF YOUR TO IT.

IT IS NOT WORTH FIGHTING THE SYMPTOMS.

ADRENALIN MAKES YOUR BODY FEEL IN DANGER.

TURN OFF SENSORING WHEN PERFORMING.

THOUGHTS ARE NOT REAL, SO DON'T REACT TO THEM.

When preparing for an audition it is helpful to have control over the problems that might arise from both yourself and others. Having the "right" thoughts and perspectives FOR YOU can ease the internal pressures and tensions before an audition. Careful phsychological preparation can make an audition a positive experience rather than a negative one.

USING FEELINGS AND EMOTIONS PRODUCTIVELY

A performer can have many different feelings in anticipation of an audition. He may feel hostility, resentment, helplessness, or fear, to name a few obvious ones. He may easily get caught up in a flood of emotions because they represent major concern and are those with which he closely identifies. Under stress he may feel like he is split into three different parts: his body, mind, and emotions.

Robert Triplett states that the prime emotions involved in stagefright are anger, fear, and confusion, and that these are born out of an inner affection for, and attraction to, the performing experience. He is saying that without an affinity for performance, a performer would have no feelings toward an audition or performance. "At the core of stagefright lies a kernel of fascination, an attraction and a commitment to performing."[2]

In learning to accept and deal with the emotions which are likely to arise in an audition situation, it is first necessary to acknowledge that they are there. Feelings are our sixth sense with the function of telling us whether what we experience is bad or good. Feelings are our reaction to that which we perceive and they in turn color and define our opinion of the world. Unfortunately, many performers find it painful to open up their feelings and use them as guides for interpreting their world. The reason for this is that the audition itself causes a person to guard against such an emotionally threatening

[2]Robert Triplett, *Stage-fright* (Chicago: Nelson-Hall, 1983) 55-56.

event. It is hard to be free when all the feelings of envy, insecurity, hurt, guilt, anger, anxiety, hope and depression all fall on our heads within the hours of the audition. The emotional turmoil that an audition causes is enough to prevent many auditioners from continuing to seek that much desired position.

David Viscott has written that if a person doesn't live in his feelings, he does not live in the real world, for feelings are the truth. The way you handle them determines whether you live in honesty or by a lie. You may discover that you use defenses to try to manage feelings. Though this may distort your perception of the truth, it does not alter that truth. You may be one who explains feelings away, but this does not resolve them or exorcise them. They are present and they must be dealt with head-on. Keep in mind that a painful feeling will not go away until it has run its natural course, for when a feeling is avoided, its painful effects are often prolonged. Dealing with it then, becomes increasingly difficult.[3]

Feelings can be viewed as signals. They can be grouped into three main emotional states:

1. SURVIVAL
   feeling anxious
   feeling guilty
   feeling ashamed
   feeling proud

2. CAUTION
   feeling upset
   feeling tired
   feeling bored
   feeling envious
   feeling used

3. SUCCESS
   feeling touched (and hurt)
   feeling moved
   feeling good

[3]David Viscott, *Risking* (New York: Simon and Schuster, 1977) 21-22.

In each of the groups there are many and diverse feelings which demand evaluation. The good feelings include pride, joy, and love, and the bad ones include guilt, despair, rage, and fear.[4]

Below are categories of emotions and feelings which may arise before, during, and after an audition. Under each heading are some insights for learning to deal with them.

ANGER

Willard Gaylin concurs with Mr. Viscott in that the most important point is to know and accept angry feelings. Acceptance of feelings, combined with the freedom to express them gives one the opportunity to decide whether or not he wishes to express those feelings. He further agrees that any emotion, such as anger, must be experienced, dissipated, and ended in order for the forgiving and forgetting process to take place.[5]

In his book, *Anger*, Leo Madow recommends the following methods which may contribute to a reasonable resolution of anger:

1. RECOGNIZE THAT YOU ARE ANGRY, admit it, then accept the fact.

2. IDENTIFY THE SOURCE OF THE ANGER. It may be perfectly obvious or you may find that it has been displaced to someone or something inappropriate.

3. UNDERSTAND WHY YOU ARE ANGRY. Upon determining this, you will be able to decide whether the reason is realistic. Anger for unrealistic reasons–usually hidden feelings, wishes, or expectations–is difficult to face and handle.

4. DEAL WITH THE ANGER REALISTICALLY. Sometimes a direct expression of anger is not always the best solution. The best way to resolve many situations is by increased communication. Decide just how realistic the anger is.[6]

Robert Triplett states that anger seeks its opposite in order to form feelings and actions into submission: CONTROL. Control conveys

---

[4]Williard Gaylin, *Feelings* (New York: Ballantine Books, 1979) 1-13.

[5]Theodore Isaac Rubin, *The Anger Book* (New York: Macmillan Publishing Co., 1969) 165.

[6]Leo Madow, *Anger* (New York: Charles Scribner's Sons, 1972) 107-23.

automatic restraint and can be the wrong answer in dealing with angry feelings. Anger's natural polarity is tranquility: "a state of energetic calmness, an attitude of vibrant composure." It displays a kind of settled strength where calmness also contains enthusiasm. Anger seeks resolution in the higher energy of compassion. Compassion gives guidance and helps to dissipate fear. It brings about a greater commitment which evolves from our inner encouragement toward excellence.[7]

CONFUSION

Confusion is often the first feeling a performer notices. There is an uncertainty about the outcome of his audition, and he is unclear about what is happening inside of himself. Not only is he unaware of his anger, but he is also unaccepting of his fear. Confusion presents itself with a spinning quality. Perhaps you have heard a friend or even yourself admit, "My head is spinning." It seems like an intellectual emotion, one that seeks to suppress the gut reactions of fear and anger, which are felt in the pit of the stomach. When we are confused, we feel jumbled up inside like an unassembled puzzle. We want to assemble the puzzle, which implies that there is an answer to the problem, even though we have not as yet figured it out.

The first step in finding an answer to confusion is to "acknowledge the quandary of confusion", states Mr. Triplett. When we devote our attention to it, we are looking for a state of focus, because confusion longs for focus and its inherent direction and order. The resulting clarity of vision enables us to see both the good and bad, that is, our mistakes and our achievements.[8]

In order to learn to handle confusion, Triplett recommends the following:

1. LIVE IN THE CONFUSION FOR A FEW MINUTES. Rather than trying to burden your mind with excessive reminders, calm it by focusing on the confusion itself. This will open a channel through which focus will be effective.

---

[7]Triplett, loc. cit., 55-61.
[8]Ibid. 67-69.

2. EXAGGERATE YOUR CONFUSION. Try to make happen exactly what you are afraid will happen. For example, simulate drawing a memory blank or forgetting a tricky fingering.

3. DON'T TRY TO THINK AWAY YOUR CONFUSION. First, you must FEEL what you feel before you can THINK about what you feel. If you think about your confusion first, you will come up with presupposed judgments about your emotions. These are usually wrong and will only end up intensifying your feelings of stagefright.[9]

FEAR

Fear stimulates the sensations of weakness, contraction, and frigidity. There is a feeling of being exposed, vulnerable, and on the brink of danger that brings with it the possibility of hurt and humiliation. Fear needs courage–courage to give in to the fear.

Accepting fear silences the stagefright voices and allows for joy. Behind its shell is found the rewards we want. Robert Triplett recommends working through fear by employing the following:

1. GIVE YOURSELF UP TO WHATEVER MIGHT HAPPEN. Take the plunge even though you have failed in your positive thinking and in controlling your feelings.

2. CHOOSE TO BE SATISFIED WITH THE WAY YOU HAVE PREPARED

3. ACCEPT WHATEVER HAPPENS IN THE PERFORMANCE.

4. HAVE THE COURAGE TO GIVE IN TO THE FEAR.[10]

GUILT

Guilt is a feeling of being unworthy, bad, evil, remorseful, self-blaming, or self-hating. Guilt can cause a person to remember only the negative events, leaving positive deeds neglected. It is the feeling that we have no right to our anger or even our feelings.

David Viscott recommends the following ways of dealing with feeling guilty:

[9]Ibid. 69-71.
[10]Ibid. 65-66.

1. YOU ALWAYS OWE YOURSELF THE TRUTH. Facing the truth about your situation is the first and often most important step in solving guilty feelings.

2. ACCEPT THE ANSWERS, HOWEVER DIFFICULT.

3. ACT IN YOUR OWN BEST INTERESTS even though you are afraid of hurting others.

4. HAVE A STRONG SENSE OF WHO YOU ARE AND WHAT YOU WANT.

5. ACCEPT THE BLAME FOR YOUR ACTIONS in order to relieve past guilt and to repair any damage you have done.

6. EXPRESS ANY ANGER OR HURT, REGARDLESS OF WHO HURT YOU. You can not afford to take on the burdens of others at the expense of your life.

7. YOU HAVE A RIGHT TO EVOLVE INTO THE BEST PERSON YOU CAN BE. No one owns you. You are here to develop and grow.[11]

DEPRESSION

Feeling "blue," "unhappy," or "down in the dumps" can describe the feeling of depression. Depression occurs when anger is trapped and turned inward. The anger becomes hatred and begins to rob life of its meaning. Energy is low and a person is sad for a long time. In order to help break the grip of depression, the following tips are recommended.

1. TURN YOUR ENERGY OUTWARD to help release trapped anger and to keep it from building up further.

2. BE HONEST WITH YOUR FEELINGS. Give up expectations of being perfect and thus the need to conceal what you feel, because what you feel is you.

3. ACCEPT THAT YOU ARE BASICALLY GOOD even if sometimes you doubt it and, what's more, can offer evidence to back up your opinion.[12]

---

[11]Viscott, loc. cit., 105-27.

4. MEDICATION CAN HELP if the depression is severe.

5. PSYCHOTHERAPY HELPS A DEPRESSED PERSON BECOME MORE SELF-AWARE and better able to cope with his problems.

6. SEE A PHYSICIAN for a complete checkup and discussion of symptoms.

7. TALK THINGS OVER with an understanding friend.

8. EXAMINE YOUR FEELINGS to figure out what is troubling you and what you can do.

9. TAKE A BREAK for a favorite activity.

10. GET SOME EXERCISE to help work off bottled up tension, to relax and to sleep better.

11. AVOID EXTRA STRESS or big changes, especially when feeling "down."[13]

HURT AND LOSS

A person might be hurt If they feel they have lost something. The more important the loss, the deeper the hurt. The defenses that help a person deal with the world do so in large part by shielding him from vulnerability to loss. Everyone feels vulnerable about something and no one ever feels totally secure, so it is best to realize that you can be hurt and proceed to be open to life. To be open means to be vulnerable–to be able to feel hurt, as well as to feel pleasure.

David Viscott recommends these thoughts in coping with loss:

1. ACCEPTING VULNERABILITY INSTEAD OF TRYING TO HIDE IT is the best way of adapting to reality.

2. DISCOVER WHAT THE LOSS MEANS TO YOU. This will help you understand the pain of the hurt and then enable you to overcome it.

3. FIND BELIEF IN YOUR OWN GOODNESS AND INNER STRENGTH. Know that no matter what comes your way, somehow you will be able to manage.

---

[12]Ibid. 128-39.

[13]Channing L. Bete Co. Inc., *About Depression* (Massachusetts: Channing L. Bete Co., 1986) 12-14.

4. USE YOUR EXPERIENCE TO HIGHLIGHT YOUR STRENGTHS AND WEAKNESSES. This process defines who you are.

5. HURT "HURTS." Accept your vulnerability and regard it as proof that you are open and sensitive to the world.

6. ACCEPT THAT YOU ARE NOT PERFECT. Stop trying to protect your image so you can be open and allowed to grow.

7. USE YOUR ENERGY TO PURSUE TRUTH AND SEARCH FOR WHAT IS BEST FOR YOU. Try not to end up justifying what is not true.

8. DECIDE THAT BEING YOUR BEST SELF IS WORTH THE PAIN AND RISK OF EXPERIENCING THE TRUTH OF YOUR FEELINGS.

9. FEELING INFERIOR IS COVERING UP FOR YOUR FEAR OF BEING HURT.

10. ANY HURT THAT IS NOT EXPRESSED LEAVES SOME PAIN INSIDE. Pain involves negative energy and depletes you of the positive energy which is used to balance out the negative.

11. TRY TO IDENTIFY THE ORIGINAL SOURCE OF LOSS and to suffer and grieve for the original loss that caused it.

12. NOTHING RESOLVES A LOSS BETTER THAN FEELING THE APPROPRIATE GRIEF OVER IT.

13. BE ENTIRELY HONEST.

14. SOME LOSSES ARE NEVER SETTLED and a person then learns to live with a sense of incompleteness and sadness.

15. WHEN YOU FEEL HURT ASK, WHAT HAVE I LOST?

16. SETTLE PROBLEMS WHEN THEY COME UP directly and honestly.

17. DO NOT EXPECT OTHER PEOPLE TO PROTECT YOU. They are here to find their way the best they can.[14]

In order to learn how to control your feelings it is important to realize that emotional misery comes from internal pressures and that

---

[14]Viscott, loc. cit., 35-52.

a person does have the ability to control or change his feelings. Albert Ellis states that a person can control his feelings by three methods:

1. YOU CAN WORK THROUGH YOUR PERCEIVING-MOVING SYSTEM. Use relaxation exercises, dancing, primal screaming or yoga breathing techniques.

2. YOU CAN COUNTERACT YOUR EXCITABILITY BY USING YOUR WILLING-THINKING PROCESS for reflecting, thinking, imaginatively desensitizing yourself, or for telling yourself calm ideas.[15]

3. YOU CAN INFLUENCE YOUR EMOTIONS BY ELECTRICAL OR BIOCHEMICAL MEANS. This can be done by taking barbiturates and tranquilizing drugs.

It is important to acknowledge what feelings appear at audition time. Being flooded with emotion before an audition should not overwhelm a person. He should, however, expect to have some feelings during this time, and the more a person cares about an event, the more emotional energy he will have invested in it.

You can not help the way you feel about things, but you can help the way you think and react to them. You may not like the reality of a situation, but you must accept it for the present moment, for in doing so, you will have control over your responses.[16]

SELF-TALK

Thoughts and feelings, are of course, integrally related. Thoughts influence our moods and shape our actions. Any thoughts we have about performance are eventually revealed in whatever performance we undertake. However, the reverse is equally true; our moods shape our thoughts, and this is where a frustrating cycle begins. The way in which we talk to ourselves, that internal dialogue that seems to always be there, has an important impact on the way we feel and think about an event. This is particularly true when we are faced with an audition

---

[15]Albert Ellis, *A New Guide to Rational Living* (New Jersey:Prentice-Hall, 1975) 19-20.
[16]Robert Anthony, *Total Self-Confidence* (San Diego: Berkley Publishing Corporation, 1979) 50.

situation. When confronted by a situation that brings on self-doubt and self-consciousness, the performer loses his perspective of OBSERVING the situation to IDENTIFYING the situation. In the latter position the performer does not see the larger picture and therefore perceives the issues of doubt, criticism, and fear as isolated entities, apart from the larger purpose. As a result, their energies change into something treacherous.[17]

There seems to be a myriad of thoughts that swirl through our heads when the pressure is felt and the adrenalin begins to flow. We have thoughts such as, "What if I let my friends and teachers down?," "If I lose this audition, I'll be out of work," "What if I blow it?," or "I'll just die on the spot." Thoughts are constant and rarely noticed, but they are powerful enough to create your most intense emotions. The internal dialogue has been called "self-talk" by rational emotive therapist Albert Ellis, and "automatic thoughts" by cognitive theorist Aaron Beck. Beck prefers the term *automatic thoughts* "because it most accurately describes the way thoughts are experienced. The person receives these thoughts as though they are by reflex–without any prior reflection or reasoning; and they impress him as plausable and valid."

Automatic thoughts usually have the following characteristics:

1. They are specific, discrete messages.

2. Automatic thoughts often appear in shorthand composed of just a few essential words or a brief visual image.

3. Automatic thoughts, no matter how irrational, are almost always believed.

4. Automatic thoughts are experienced as spontaneous and pop into your mind.

5. Automatic thoughts are often couched in terms of should, ought, or must.

6. Automatic thoughts tend to "awfulize."

7. Automatic thoughts are relatively idiosyncratic.

8. Automatic thoughts are hard to turn off.

---

[17]Triplett, loc. cit., 29.

9. Automatic thoughts are learned.[18]

Conscious self-criticism makes one do worse. This has been proven by Dr. E. Collon Cherry of London, England. Writing in the British scientific journal *Nature*, Dr. Cherry stated his belief that stuttering was caused by "excessive monitoring." To test his theory he equipped twenty-five severe stutterers with earphones through which a loud tone drowned out the sound of their own voices. When asked to read aloud from a prepared text under these conditions, which eliminated self-criticism, the improvement was "remarkable." When excessive negative feedback, or self-criticism, was eliminated, inhibition disappeared and performance improved. When there was no time to worry, or too much carefulness in advance, expression immediately improved. This gives us a valuable clue as to how we may release a pent up personality, and improve performance in other areas.[19]

Unlike other animals, people tell themselves various sane and crazy things. Their beliefs, attitudes, opinions and philosophies largely take the form of internalized sentences or self-talk.[20] In relation to anxiety management this means that because we tell ourselves a) I might make a mistake and fall on my face before this group of people and b) I have to think it AWFUL if I do make a mistake and fall on my face in public, these catastrophic sentences almost immediately begin to make us feel anxious.[21]

This principle finds its roots in ancient Greek and Roman philosophers, notably the famous stoic Epictetus, who in the first century A.D. wrote in the *Enchiridion*: "Men feel disturbed not by things, but by the views which they take of them." William Shakespeare, many centuries later, rephrased this thought in *Hamlet*: "There exists nothing either good or bad but thinking makes it so. . . ."[22]

What do we do with these good and bad voices in our heads? Perhaps the most important thing to remember is: DO NOT FIGHT YOUR

---

[18]Matthew McKay, *Thoughts and Feelings* (California: New Harbinger Publications, 1981) 14.

[19]Maxwell Maltz, *Psycho-Cybernetics* (New York: Prentice-Hall, Inc., 1980) 172.

[20]Ellis, loc. cit., x.

[21]Ibid. 10.

[22]Ibid. 33.

THOUGHTS. The more you resist your thoughts, the more they will get in your way. However, once you stop resisting them and let them pass by without giving them your full attention, they will stop intruding.[23] All techniques for conscious control involve AFFIRMING that whatever is desired already exists and VISUALIZING the current existence of that desired. The difference between affirmation and visualization is that the former is a verbal statement, and the latter a mental picture. In using positive affirmation and visualization as tools for conscious creation, remember to allow for resistance. There is a part of us (unconscious beliefs) that does not want us to have that which we consciously desire. If we let them babble out all the reasons why we should not have what we want, they gradually disappear.[24] As Meister Eckhart said, "We must let go of who we think we are in order to be the person we can become."

In Robert Triplett's book, *Stage-fright* we learn that pinpointing stagefright voices helps us see what qualities they possess, what messages they send out, and what part they play in the internal drama. The Critic voice desires an absolute standard represented by the Perfectionist, the Doubter seeks the guarantee of success promised by the Dogmatist, and the Weakling craves the Protector's defensive shield.[25] These Subpersonalities chatter freely in our heads, commenting on nearly everything that happens to us in our waking moments. Often, however, conversation takes place between those that are dually opposed.[26]

Often stress brings on distorted thinking. Dr. McKay cites fifteen styles of distorted thinking in his book, *Thoughts and Feelings*:

1. FILTERING: You take the negative details and magnify them while filtering out all the positive aspects of a situation.

2. POLARIZED THINKING: Things are black or white, good or bad. You have to be perfect or you are a failure. There is no middle ground.

---

[23]Anthony, loc. cit., 146.

[24]Elizabeth Brenner, *Winning By Letting Go* (San Diego: Harcourt Brace Jovanovich, 1985) 82.

[25]Triplett, loc. cit. 31

[26]Ibid. 22.

3. OVERGENERALIZATION: You come to a general conclusion based on a single incident or piece of evidence. If something bad happens once, you expect it to happen over and over again.

4. MIND READING: Without them saying so, you know what people are feeling and why they act the way they do. In particular, you are able to define how people are feeling toward you.

5. CATASTROPHIZING: You expect disaster. You notice or hear about a problem and start "what ifs" : What if tragedy strikes? What if it happens to you?

6. PERSONALIZATION: You think that everything people do or say is some kind of reaction to you. You also compare yourself to others, trying to determine who is smarter, better looking, etc.

7. CONTROL FALLACIES: If you feel externally controlled, you see yourself as a helpless a victim of fate. The fallacy of internal control has you responsible for the pain and happiness of everyone around you.

8. FALLACY OF FAIRNESS. You feel resentful because you think you know what is fair but other people will not agree with you.

9. BLAMING: You hold other people responsible for your pain, or take the other tack and blame yourself for every problem or reversal.

10. SHOULDS: You have a list of ironclad rules about how you and other people should act. People who break the rules anger you and.you feel guilty if you violate the rules.

11. EMOTIONAL REASONING: You believe that what you feel must be automatically true. If you feel stupid and boring, then you must BE stupid and boring.

12. FALLACY OF CHANGE: You expect that other people will change to suit you if you just pressure or cajole them enough. You need to change people because your hopes for happiness seem to depend entirely on them.

13. GLOBAL LABELING: You generalize one or two qualities into a negative global judgement.

14. BEING RIGHT: You are continually on trial to prove that your opinions and actions are correct. Being wrong is unthinkable and you will go to any length to demonstrate your rightness.

15. HEAVEN'S REWARD FALLACY: You expect all your sacrifice and self-denial to pay off, as if there were someone keeping score. You feel bitter when the reward is not there.[27]

If you are not in the habit of listening to your thoughts, it is hard to catch your distorted thinking. "The best tipoff that you are using a distorted thinking style is the presence of painful emotions. You feel nervous, depressed or chronically angry. You play certain worries over and over like a broken record."[28]

Once you can recognize that your thoughts are affecting you, try to combat their harmful effects by:

1. Naming your emotion;

2. Describing the situation or event;

3. Identifying your distortions; and

4. Eliminating your distortions.[29]

In learning to eliminate your distortions it is important to have key comeback statements. Since the thoughts that pop in are short phrases, the comeback phrase should also be short. McKay suggests the following:

1. Filtering–SHIFT FOCUS, NO NEED TO MAGNIFY.

2. Polarized Thinking–NO BLACK AND WHITE JUDGEMENTS. THINK IN PERCENTAGES.

3. Overgeneralization–QUANTIFY; IS THERE EVIDENCE FOR CONCLUSIONS? THERE ARE NO ABSOLUTES.

4. Mind-reading–CHECK IT OUT; IS THERE EVIDENCE FOR CONCLUSIONS?

5. Catastrophizing–REALISTIC ODDS.

[27]McKay, loc. cit., 26.
[28]Ibid. 34.
[29]Ibid. 35.

6. Personalization–CHECK IT OUT, IS THERE EVIDENCE FOR CONCLUSIONS? WHY RISK COMPARISIONS?

7. Control Fallacies.–I MAKE IT HAPPEN; EACH PERSON IS RESPONSIBLE.

8. Fallacy of Fairness–PREFERENCE vs. FAIRNESS.

9. Blaming–I MAKE IT HAPPEN, EACH ONE IS RESPONSIBLE.

10. Shoulds–FLEXIBLE RULES, FLEXIBLE VALUES.

11. Emotional Reasoning–FEELINGS CAN LIE.

12. Fallacy of Change–I MAKE IT HAPPEN.

13. Global Reasoning–BE SPECIFIC.

14. Being Right–ACTIVE LISTENING.

15. Heaven's Reward Fallacy–THE REWARD IS NOW.[30]

When you can recognize your automatic thoughts and come back with a short quick phrase in order to neutralize them, the next step is to assess them. McKay recommends you inventory them as follows:

1. SENSIBLE. This is quite a sensible and reasonable thing for me to think.

2. HABIT. This is just a habit. I think it automatically, without really worrying about it.

3. NOT NECESSARY. I often realize that this thought is not really necessary, but I don't try to stop it.

4. TRY TO STOP. I know this thought is not necessary. It bothers me and I must try to stop it.

5. TRY VERY HARD TO STOP IT. This thought upsets me a great deal and I try very hard to stop it.[31]

Rating these stressful thoughts in relation to how they interfere with your performance is also important in order to gain perspective on them:

[30]Ibid. 44.
[31]Ibid. 48.

92

1. NO INTERFERENCE. This thought does not interfere with my activities.

2. INTERFERES A LITTLE. This thought interferes a little with my activities or wastes a little of my time.

3. INTERFERES MODERATELY. This thought interferes with my activities or wastes my time.

4. INTERFERES A GREAT DEAL. This thought stops me from doing a lot of things and wastes a lot of time each day.[32]

Another way to help rid yourself of unwanted thoughts is by using a technique called "thought stoppage." This works when you catch yourself dwelling on your distressing thoughts and you consciously shout to yourself "STOP!!!" This helps you gain control over your mind and get back the concentration you wanted before the unwanted thoughts popped in.

Practicing thought interruption creates a hole or vacuum. As soon as you interrupt one train of thought, another seems to step right in and take its place. You can take advantage of this phonomenon by selecting effective substitute non-stressful thoughts. In an audition environment, anxious thoughts seem to come in four distinct phases:

1. Anticipatory anxiety–experienced when getting ready for or thinking about a stressful situation or event.

2. Initial confrontation–when you first experience whatever you fear.

3. Trying to cope–experienced during the event.

4. Looking back and worrying–hindsight to see how well you did.

To cope with these four phases of anxiety, it is helpful to prepare things to say to yourself before, at the beginning, during, and after potentially disturbing situations. Some ideas are as follows:

BEFORE THE EVENT

Worrying won't make it any different.

What exactly do you have to do?

---

[32]Ibid. 49.

Just think rationally. Negative thoughts are not normal.

You can plan how to deal with it.

BEGINNING OF THE EVENT

Just get a grip on yourself. You can handle this.

You only have to take it one step at a time.

Keep your mind on what you have to do, not on the fear.

This anxiety is a signal to relax.

DURING THE EVENT

Take a deep breath, pause, and relax.

What is the next step? Focus on that.

Fear is natural. It arises and subsides, and you can keep it under control.

It will be over soon. Nothing lasts forever.

Worse things could happen.

Do something to take your mind off your fear.

AFTER THE EVENT

You did it!

That wasn't so bad.

It's getting easier.

You could do it again with half the trouble.

Your thoughts about it were worse that the thing itself.

Once again you were bigger than your fear.

This really works.[33]

Talking back to your automatic thoughts can bring relief to unwanted and self-sabatoging messages from your subconscious mind.

---

[33]Ibid. 52.

When thoughts of anger or depression crop in, saying these covert assertions can be helpful:

You're strong enough to handle criticism.

Expect less from them and then you can calm down.

Take a deep breath. In an hour it won't matter.

Life is not fair.

Go slow and see it from their perspective.

Memories make you feel worse.

Decide something, one way or the other.

Think about what you can do right now.

Say good-bye to the past.

Look for what you like about you.

It's OK to forget about the past.[34]

SYSTEMATIC DESENSITIZATION was a technique developed by behavior therapist Joseph Wolpe in 1958. His early technique trained people to relax progressively in order to inhibit high levels of anxiety. Two basic principles underlay Systematic Desensitzation:

1. One emotion can be used to counteract another; and

2. Threatening situations can be gotten used to.[35]

In order to master this technique, one must learn to physically relax. Deep breathing, muscle relaxation, mental imagery all help to loosen the grip of tension. Having an understanding of how to quickly relax the four major muscle groups can be a major advantage at times of stress. Repeating the relaxation techniques will enable you to give your body a sign to relax on a moment's notice. When systematically going through your hierarchy of stress-producing images (the stages of auditioning), you can intermingle both the stressful image and the relaxation technique. Once you are able to keep relaxed while picturing your worse fears, you will find that this technique transfers to real life situations.

[34]Ibid. 54.
[35]Ibid. 77.

Donald Meichenbaum developed a technique of relaxing through self-talk, called STRESS INOCULATION. In his book, *Cognitive Behavior* he suggests the following four steps for coping with any stressful situation:

1. PREPARING

    There's nothing to worry about.

    I'm going to be all right.

    I've succeeded with this before.

    What exactly do I have to do?

    I know I can do each one of these tasks.

    It's easier once I get started.

    I'll jump in and be all right.

    Tomorrow I'll be through it.

    Don't let negative thoughts creep in.

2. CONFRONTING THE STRESSFUL SITUATION

    Stay organized.

    Take it step by step, don't rush.

    I can do this, I am doing it now.

    I can only do my best.

    Any tension I feel is a signal to use my coping exercises.

    I can get help If I need it.

    If I don't talk about fear I won't be afraid.

    If I get tense, I'll take a breather and relax.

    It's OK to make mistakes.

3. COPING WITH EMOTIONAL AROUSAL

    Relax now!

    Just breathe deeply.

    There's an end to it.

    Keep my mind on right now, on the present task at hand.

    I can keep this within limits I can handle.

    I am only afraid because I decided to be. I can decide not to be.

    I've survived this and worse before.

Being active will lessen the fear.

4. REINFORCING SUCCESS
I did it!
I did it all right. I did well.
Next time I won't have to worry as much.
I am going to relax away anxiety.
It's possible not to be scared. All I have to do is stop thinking I'm scared.[36]

VISUALIZATION is a powerful tool used to gain control of your mind, emotions, and body for bringing about desired changes in your behavior. It is used to create a blueprint which can positively modify your life.

A more structured way of consulting with your blueprint, is to have an inner guide. Your inner guide is a wise and helpful messenger who has access to the rich storehouse of knowledge in your unconscious mind. Your inner guide may take many forms: a person, an animal, a plant, a place or an event. The inner guide may speak, demonstrate, point out, or simply allude to the answer you are looking for. To consult this guide it is necessary to relax enough so to enter your 'special place' and ask it questions and wait for it to answer.[37]

Visualizing your goals and how you want to act can program you to respond in desired ways. Gaining this type of control can be a great help at auditions where auotmatic thoughts of bad outcomes tend to dampen chances of success.

A technique called COVERT REINFORCEMENT can be used to approach situations which you previously avoided out of fear. It involves pairing your negative behavior or feelings with a positive reinforcer. Instructions for applying this technique are:

1. DESCRIBE YOUR AVOIDANCE BEHAVIOR - Your avoidance behavior is what you do that is a problem for you.

2. DESCRIBE YOUR APPROACH BEHAVIOR. Your approach behavior is what you want to happen.

[36]Ibid. 99.
[37]Ibid. 124.

3. LIST YOUR POSITIVE REINFORCERS. Positive reinforcers are pleasant situations or experiences that you can enjoy, easily imagine, create good feelings about, and can easily erase from your mind at will.

4. PRACTICE REAXATION. This helps clear the mind.

5. PRACTICE IMAGINING REINFORCERS. Try to use all five senses.

6. RECORD YOUR APPROACH BEHAVIOR SCENE. Tape record the scene to help you clearly recreate it at will.

7. LISTEN TO YOUR APPROACH BEHAVIOR SCENE. This step puts all the steps together. Select for your reinforcer an enjoyable scene that is easy to visualize and relax as you listen to your fear-producing scene. While putting yourself fully into the stressful situation, recreate the enjoyable scene for about 20 seconds, then erase it and relax as the description of the negative scene continues.

8. USE COVERT REINFORCEMENT IN REAL LIFE. When you feel comfortable rehearsing your approach behavior scene you are ready to put it into practice in real life.[38]

An effective way of altering an existing negative sequence of behavior, or of learning a new behavior pattern is called COVERT MODELING. In auditions where one might feel alot of anxiety, this technique can help one learn a new way of reacting.

> One of the most important ways that you learn to perform a new behavior is to observe and imitate someone else doing it successfully. A young musician may learn to perform on stage by watching his favorite artists on television or at concerts, and then modeling his behavior after theirs.[39]

In order to utilize COVERT MODELING this approach is used:

1. Write out your problem behavior.

2. Write out your desired behavior.

---

[38]Ibid. 145.
[39]Ibid. 151.

3. Practice imagining the context where the problem behavior occurs.

4. Imagine someone very different performing your desired behavior.

5. Imagine someone similar to you performing your desired behavior with difficulty first, then successfully.

6. Imagine yourself performing the desired behavior and gradually mastering it. See yourself performing perfectly twice.

7. Role play your desired behavior in front of a mirror and then in front of friends.

8. Prepare some coping statements before, during and after the event.

9. Perform the desired behavior in real life.[40]

Another approach used in behavior modification is called PARADOXICAL INTENTION. This approach is the least understood and used when most other approaches fail. What you try to achieve in this therapy is to dare yourself to fail in the task. In an audition you would try and make your worst fears happen. There are twelve rules to follow when playing the "paradox game."

1. Forget trying to understand the process.

2. Determine the symptom-solution cycle. Descibe the symptom as an action so you can think of your fear in precise physical discomfort.

3. Discourage resistance–try to hide how you feel.

4. Define good behavior. Set clear models on how you would like to behave in the situation.

5. Secure a commitment to change. Make a solid pact with yourself.

6. Set a time limit–have a deadline to add pressure.

---

[40]Ibid. 155.

7. Prescribe the symptom. Tell yourself to do the thing that bothers you, such as telling insomniacs to stay up all night, or order fainters to fall down, or instruct perfectionists to make mistakes.

8. Include a variation. Allow some small changes in doing the thing that you are afraid of, such as letting the perfectionist make calculated, small mistakes instead of just the big catastrophic ones.

9. Reframe your language. Look at the event in a different light and use new words to describe it.

10. Secure an agreement to follow instructions.

11. Predict a relapse. Remember that progress is not always in a straight line, you are still in control.

12. De-mystify and/or Disengage–try to understand what has happened.[41]

The manner in which a person talks to himself can exert a huge influence on his performance in an audition situation. The low self-esteem brought on by self-defeating thoughts, putdowns and the feelings of unworthiness and guilt, can be eased by talking back to your automatic thoughts. Try not to let negative thoughts have the last word.

CONCENTRATION AND ATTENTIONAL SHIFTS

A major problem in auditioning is being able to keep our minds on the music we are performing. The mind tends to wander and sabotage our playing with distractions. Sometimes it is that little voice in our head that rots away our self-confidence, and other times it may be the tension in our body which causes such distracting sensations. However a distraction manifests itself, it keeps one from staying in the present

---

[41]Ibid. 188.

moment and from feeling in control. It therefore contributes to the overall problem of concentration. It may be worthwhile to review both the chapters on Self-talk and Relaxation Techniques if this is a particular trouble area for you.

Man has to provide the goal of his mental activity with the ability to control his awareness. This requires focusing the mind on awareness, which acts as the regulator and integrator of one's mental activity. Nathaniel Branden says in his book, *The Psychology of Self-Esteem* that "The goal of awareness is set by giving oneself the order: "grasp this.""

This order is not automatic and must be set into operation by a man's consciousness. Sustaining that focus with regard to a specific issue or problem, is simply done by thinking. To let one's mind drift in will-less passivity, directed only by random impressions, emotions or associations; or to consider an issue without genuinely seeking to understand it; or to engage in an action without being concerned about what one is doing, are all examples of being out of focus.

There are different levels of awareness possible to an individual's mind, as determined by an individual's degree of focus. This will manifest itself in:

1. the clarity or vagueness of his mind's contents;

2. the degree to which the mind's activity involves abstractions and principles or is concrete-bound; and

3. the degree to which the relevant wider context is present or absent in the process of thinking.

What this implies is that the choice to think is a process of moving from a lower level of awareness to a higher level; that is, to move from mental passivity to purposeful mental activity, thereby initiating a process of directed awareness.[42]

Here is a list of thoughts and discoveries which will help control the mind, in pursuit of improving your condition:

1. TO LET YOUR MIND DRIFT IS TO BE OUT OF FOCUS and you are choosing unawareness as your goal.

[42]Nathaniel Braden, *The Psychology of Self-Esteem* (New York: Bantam Books, 1981) 40-41.

2. CHOOSE AN OBJECT OR EVENT TO FOCUS ON and you will be in control.

3. KNOW WHAT YOUR MIND IS DOING and you will be in focus.

4. LETTING YOUR MIND DRIFT BRINGS UP FEELINGS of helplessness and anxiety, and you have the sense of living in an unknowable and inimcal universe. It undercuts confidence and the ability to think.[43]

5. FIND SOMETHING WHICH HOLDS YOUR INTEREST. Be enthusiastic and your incentive will automatically be increased.

6. TRY AND REMEMBER HOW YOU WANT TO PERFORM. This will require use of your thinking ability in dealing with slippling into the past, yet directing it toward a past goal.

7. ANTICIPATE THE RESULTS OF YOUR INTENTION. This uses your thinking ability to plan ahead.

8. PONDER ON YOUR PERFORMING. This will lock you into the present and give continuous thought enabling you to solve a problem or to understand something.

9. THINK CREATIVELY. Use your imagination to find more interest in what you are doing.

10. DO NOT OTHER THOUGHT TO ENTER YOUR MIND. Strive to fix your mind on an object and hang on to it.[44]

11. SHIFT INTO OBSERVING YOURSELF INSTEAD OF PARTICIPATING IN YOUR CIRCUMSTANCES. Be an objective observer and notice the sense of perspective you gain.[45]

12. ALLOW YOUR NATURAL ABILITIES TO EXPRESS THEMSELVES. Trust this "unthinking state" without trying to control and manipulate it.[46]

13. ACCEPT YOUR LOSS OF CONCENTRATION AND GO ON. Re-focus yourself by thinking of your original object.

[43]Ibid. 42-46.
[44]Harry Lorayne, *Secrets of Mind Power* (New York: Signet, 1975) 1-111.
[45]Brenner, loc. cit., 7.
[46]Barry Green, *The Inner Game of Music* (New York: Anchor Press, 1986) 21.

14. YOU CAN ONLY THINK OF ONE THING AT A TIME. This will give you confidence when you seek to gain control over your concentration.

15. YOU CAN CO-EXIST WITH INTERFERENCE. Extraneous diversions will be less of a diversion if you accept the interference

When it is dIfficult to concentrate on your performance, remember that there are ways to gain control over those distractions which hamper you. Learning to remain in a focused, concentrated, and involved state of mind can be the key to a successful audition.

RELAXATION TECHNIQUES

In order to control the pressures and stresses of auditioning, it is important to be able to relax when we need to. When our personal fears concerning auditions manifest themselves in furrowed brows, clenched fists, knotted stomachs and tense muscles, physical symptoms command our attention. Not only do our thoughts affect our body, but, similarly, our body influences our thoughts and feelings. It can become a vicious circle if one does not know how to control the spiral which may occur.

Much of the time, the physical state our bodies are in can be a determining factor of our level of stagefright. The stagefright response or the "fight-or-flight" instinct arises in our reacting to a threat to our self-concept and an involuntary dramatic shift of body energies occurs to prepare for protective action, thus producing an array of physical symptoms.[47]

Robert Triplett says that in order to effectively counteract the effects of tension, it is necessary to neutralize them. This entails elongating muscles, opening electrical blocks, regulating breathing, reducing brain-wave activity, and developing a keen kinesthetic awareness so that we can determine what neutralizing steps should be taken. A good plan to combat the effects of tension ought to include:

---

[47]Triplett, loc. cit., 115.

1. giving the performer a greater kinesthetic sense of his body;

2. promoting advanced relaxation; and

3. showing how to build from a state of advanced relaxation to one that is energized enough for an exciting performance.[48]

Should you wish to experiment with the various methods of relaxation, below are presented some techniques and ideas from a variety of sources.

1. LABEL YOUR TENSION FROM 1-10. By monitoring the tension on a scale from 1-10 (1 being the most relaxed and 10 being a great deal of tension), and knowing what level you are at, try to deliberately increase it and then relax back to your original tension. By relaxing you should be able to notice what muscles get in the way and you will then have more control over your tension level.[49]

2. TENSE AND RELAX. Lie on the floor and tighten each part of your body. Hold the tension until you are rigid from the bottoms of your feet to the top of your head. Then, from the top of your head, slowly start relaxing each part of your body by degrees, until you have reached your toes. This forces your muscles to relax by tiring them and teaches you to recognize the varying degrees of tension in your body.

3. MAKE YOURSELF FEEL LOGY. Lie on the floor and become aware of your own body weight. Slowly exaggerate your weight until you feel much heavier. Feel the pull of gravity.[50]

4. LISTEN. Listen to whatever sound you hear. Pick out each sound and separate it from other sounds. It not only takes you outside of yourself and your own concerns, but it also heightens your sensory awareness so as to relax the other parts of you.

5. LOOK. Make a conscious effort to see things you have not seen before. You will be easing your audition fears by heightening your sensory awareness and getting outside of yourself.

[48]Ibid. 117.
[49]Green, loc. cit., 4-5.
[50]Eric Morris, *Being and Doing* (California: Spelling Publications, 1981) 20-21.

6. FEEL. Feel the temperature of the room and the texture of your clothes. Be aware of how things feel.

7. TASTE. If your mouth is dry, be aware of how that tastes. If you have just had water, taste the dampness.

8. SMELL. Be aware of the smell of the room or the perfume of someone around you. Learn to expand yourself to the size of the world. At the same time you will be opening yourself up, making yourself more receptive, and more aware, and also helping to loosen those muscles which tense up when there is an abundance of self-concern, and prevents you from doing your freest and most creative work.

9. EXERCISE. Physical warm-ups, like some sit-ups, leg-ups, knee-bends, toe-raises, and a little jogging will wake you up and get you in control of your body, instead of the other way around. The purpose of these exercises is to stimulate you and to relax cramped and tightened muscles.

10. BREATHE. Inhale 5 counts, hold 10 counts, and exhale 10 counts. Be conscious of the air going in, what it does when it is in there, and how it goes out.

11. MAKE SIGHING SOUNDS. After a few deep breaths, exhale; while exhaling, allow sound to be added to the breath, so it becomes a long sigh. After a few sighs, make this exhaling sound into the different vowel sounds, one at a time, exaggerating what the face does to make the "AA," "EE," "I," "OO" sounds.[51]

12. GIVE YOURSELF A LOT OF TIME BEFORE THE AUDITION. Avoid making yourself feel frazzled by having to rush to get there.[52]

13. PRETEND YOU ARE NEEDED BY THE COMMITTEE. Pretend that you are walking into a room of people who need your warmth and affection, and who could not possibly threaten you. Practice this exercise daily until you can turn this acting adjustment on

---

[51]Gordon Hunt, *How to Audition* (New York: Harper and Row, 1977) 58-60.
[52]Tome Markus, *The Professional Actor* (New York: Drama Book Specialists, 1979) 135.

and off whenever you want. A good audition is a rehearsed, top-notch performance that looks spontaneous, but that can be summoned at will.

14. PRETEND YOU OWN THE BUILDING AND THEATRE. Imagine how you would feel if the people who are running the audition owed you three month's back rent. Practice this and you can turn on a sense of authority and power at will and feel relaxed about the future.[53]

15. AWARENESS BREATHING.

A. Take a break. Think about what is causing you to feel tense and then put these thoughts out of your mind.

B. Relax your arms and shoulders.

C. Slowly exhale through your nose.

D. Take a deep breath, letting your abdomen and then your chest fill with air.

E. Exhale slowly and repeat until your breathing is regular and steady. As you do, concentrate on each breath.

F. Feel relaxed and in control.

16. A QUICK METHOD.

A. Relax your arms and shoulders.

B. Rotate your head in a circle a few times, first to the right, then to the left.

C. Close your eyes. Take a deep breath and exhale.

Repeat.

D. Concentrate on your breathing, putting aside all stressful thoughts.[54]

17. MEDITATION. Use the techniques of meditation to relax your mind and then your body.

18. BIOFEEDBACK. Biofeedback training uses special medical instruments to measure the amount of stress in your body. A

[53]Fred Silver, *Auditioning for the Musical Theatre* (New York: Newmarket Press, 1985) 106-07.
[54]Channing L. Bete Co., Inc., *About Stress Management* (Massachusetts: Channing L. Bete Co., 1986) 9.

skilled instructor can help you use this information to control your reaction to stress and help you relax.

19. HYPNOSIS. This technique can be used to bring about a relaxed, stress-free state in a person. It can be used to break other stress-related habits such as smoking, alcohol and drug abuse.

20. FELDENKRAIS. This is a series of movement lessons which teaches us to move with less effort and to free the neck, joints and breathing.

21. ALEXANDER TECHNIQUE. Through this technique, we learn how to align the body and the skeletal structure.

22. VISUALIZATION. Soothe strained nerves by taking an imaginary trip to an ideal place. Close your eyes, take a deep breath, and for the next 10 minutes imagine yourself in any desirable place.[55]

23. GET ENOUGH SLEEP. This will help ensure you can meet each day's challenges with energy and alertness.

24. TALK OUT WORRIES. Talking with a trusted friend can go a long way toward putting your problems in perspective.

25. MANAGE YOUR TIME WISELY. Make a list of things to do each day so you can keep your routine orderly and efficient. Do not try to do everything at once. Plan realistic goals.

26. TAKE A BREAK. Take a break from what you are doing once in a while so you can feel refreshed and relaxed.[56]

27. HAVE SOME FUN. Recreation allows you to transfer your stressed mental state into other areas of the self.

28. TAKE A WALK. Twenty minutes of walking is very effective at reducing stress.

29. TRY A MASSAGE. With the physical method of massage, the muscles and tendons, joints, skin and fatty tissues are manipulated. The primary purpose is to relieve partial muscle contractions (knots) and subsequently induce relaxation.

[55]Ibid. 11.
[56]Ibid. 12.

30. TAKE A HOT BATH. Prolonged heat can relax the muscles and "clean" the worries out of your mind.

31. BREATHE SLOWER. Slow your breathing process to a 7-second inhale and an 8-second exhale.

32. HAVE A GOOD CRY. Tears can help relieve stress by ridding the body of potentially harmful chemicals produced during stressful times and can be a soothing emotional outlet.

33. LEARN TO PRAY. To the followers of religion, be conscious of the meaning of the words. The most effective prayers involve the body and the mind as well as the spirit working together.[57]

In his book, *Stage-fright*, Robert Triplett offers a five-day program for attuning the body and inducing a state of relaxation. Here is an outline of that program.

DAY ONE

SCAN YOUR BODY to provide a basic awareness of your whole system and how it feels.

HORIZONTAL NECK ROLLS to loosen and elongate neck muscles. DOWNWARD STRETCHES of your left and right arms. Finish session by scanning the body to observe any new changes in the body. Observe any new looseness of your muscles.

DAY TWO

DEAD REPOSE induces advanced relaxation by conscious tensing of the muscles and subsequent release. With each inhalation gradually tense the muscles listed below, and with each exhalation gradually release the tension.

EYEBROWS

LIPS

JAW

NECK

LEFT ARM

---

[57]Authors of the Rodale Press, *21 Surefire Stress Releasers* (Pennsylvania: Rodale Press, 1983) 10-13.

RIGHT ARM
CHEST
LOWER ABDOMEN
BUTTOCKS
LEFT LEG
RIGHT LEG
ENTIRE BODY

Lie quietly for a few minutes.

HORIZONTAL SHOULDER RELAXATION loosens the muscles in the neck, shoulders, and the upper back.

HIP RELAXATION elongates the muscles and opens up the electrical systems of the body.

DAY THREE

BODY SCAN to get a sense of the body tension.

FULL HORIZONTAL STRETCH

VERTICAL ARCS to stretch the back, pelvis, legs and feet.

ELONGATING NECK AND UPPER BACK

PELVIC STRETCH to loosen and elongate the muscles of the lower back.

EXTENDED PELVIC STRETCH.

THE BREATHING BODY reduces tension in the diaphragm and facilitates your ability to sense the body's electrical energy system.

DAY FOUR

UPRIGHT BODY SCAN to find a natural standing posture.

FLUTTER BREATHING to release blocked energy held by the diaphragm.

UPRIGHT BODY STRETCH.

THE WINDMILL.

THE CORKSCREW to free the lower half of the body.

THE BODY SHAKE to calm the body down and become more vibrant.

THE WALKING BODY SCAN to see how you move when you feel calm and vibrant. Take pleasure in the way you walk.

DAY FIVE

NECK ROLLS

DANGLING HEAD TURNS

BOUNCING BEND

BACK STRETCH

BODY QUIVER

CREATING NEW SENSATIONS by experimenting with other feelings to lay over the fundamental one of repose.

Let the body wind down afterwards and feel the quiet awareness you have generated. Then think of a feeling to integrate with this awareness, one which you find valuable to your performance circumstances, such as: joy, humor, daring, power, clarity, vibrance, focus, vitality, compassion, wonder, grandeur, nimbleness, playfulness. In a relaxed state, see what area of the body begins to stir when the added feeling is evoked. In attuning the body, its innate resources are discovered and this brings a feeling of enthusiasm while revealing a sense of autonomy. With this we gain the ability to utilize the power we discovered and in turn have created the specific energy we need for a performance.[58]

HUMOR

In searching out ways in which to cope with the pressures of auditioning, the use of humor is often overlooked. Survival requires a sense of humor about our place in the divine scheme of things and a true belief that we are evolving, that is, always becoming something better than we were before.[59]

---

[58]Triplett, loc. cit. 115-50.
[59]Silver, loc. cit., 171.

It is important to have a sense of humor, because it can act as a safety valve. While it keeps you from taking yourself too seriously, it also relieves your tensions.[60] Since humor allows us to laugh at our fears, we should not be afraid of going too far in our interpretations. Just as in life, when we go or someone else goes too far, we tend to laugh. Learn to take the risk.

Humor is not just being funny and it is not just telling jokes. We use humor to lighten the burden for ourselves and others because of the weight we are dumping on ourselves and on them. The heavier the situation, the more we need humor to endure it.[61]

Rollo May points out that it is not generally realized how closely one's sense of humor is connected with one's sense of selfhood. Humor should normally have the function of preserving the sense of self. It is the healthy way of feeling a "distance" between one's self and one's problem with perspective. One cannot laugh when in an anxiety panic, for then one is swallowed up, having lost the distinction between himself and the world around him. "So long as one can laugh, furthermore, he is not completely under the domination of anxiety or fear and hence the accepted belief in folklore that to be able to laugh in times of danger is a sign of courage."[62]

Humor, like anything else in the human mind, can be positive, negative, hostile, gentle, and so forth. When one removes himself from reality and views the human condition from above, that is, with objective indifference, one can really appreciate the value of humor. Humor, then, is what allows us to objectify and take less seriously the basic requirements of life on our planet with all other humans.[63]

There are many ways in which one can objectify human life if he penetrates deeply enough inside his true self, abandoning the outside activities with which he is identified. In so doing, he is able to realize his true self as independent of the human condition as generally presented. The humor as a direct experience becomes increasingly frequent.[64] When we laugh in anger or rage we are feeling a vindictive type of humor. We laugh because we are triumphant over others, rather than because we

---

[60]Anthony, loc. cit., 169-70.
[61]Michael Shurtleff, *Audition* (New York: Bantam Books, 1978) 74-75.
[62]Rollo May, *Man's Search for Himself* (New York: Delta Books, 1973) 62-63.
[63]John Lilly, *Simulations of God* (New York: Simon and Schuster, 1975) 179-81.
[64]Ibid. 181.

have gone a step further toward our own achievement.[65] Anger may come out more directly and in socially acceptable forms such as sarcasm and biting humor. These are ways that anger is acted out, anger with which we can identify because it is present in all of us but which becomes overt. As human beings, we tend to enjoy that which represents our hidden wishes.[66]

For the most part, humor is based on incongruities of one sort or another. If a person is unable to assess the degree of incongruity he will not appreciate the humor.[67] Knowing what it is that we fear or take too seriously can make us aware of that material we have at our disposal of which we can make fun.

In Carlos Castaneda's *A Separate Reality*, the author states that Don Juan presents a nonsensical "intellectual position" which in a way encompasses the idea of "controlled folly." As Don Juan "sees" it, all of his actions are folly because each thing is as important as everything else; no one thing matters more than any other. His acts of controlled folly are at one and the same time totally sincere and yet always the acts of an actor. In fact, all of Don Juan's acts are controlled folly, he says, because he does everything even while "seeing" its unimportance.[68] How is this nonsense related to humor?

Luke Rhinehart answers this question by saying that enlightenment and humor are almost always linked. One can rarely have an enlightenment experience except under the impact of nonsense. Every time we laugh we are in a way experiencing a mini-enlightenment, a tiny letting go of an attachment to some bit of belief or sense. Full enlightenment, in these terms, is accepting what is, which leads to experiencing fully whatever one is experiencing.[69]

Eloise Ristad, in her book, *A Soprano on Her Head*, speaks of overcoming the effects of internal judges by using your sense of humor to make fun of them. She cites an example:

---

[65]Ibid. 63.

[66]Madow, 12.

[67]Edward Hall, *The Silent Language* (New York: Fawcett World Library, 1959) 123-24.

[68]Luke Rhinehart, *The Book of EST* (New York: Holt, Rinehart and Winston, 1976) 248.

[69]Ibid. 249.

In one session, a young woman giggled out loud as her judges, all of them familiar characters from her everyday life, grew long noses. In the next session we used her image, but first dressed our judges in long, dignified robes. As we imagined them growing long noses, we also stripped them of their robes and watched them scurry for cover, completely naked. As we laughed them away we realized that they had lost some of their power.[70]

In the same book she points out that when someone plays clown and helps us find the humor in a predicament, we find delightful flips from one possibility to another and also gain perspective. When we try to enjoy the situation we find ourselves in, we can turn our moods around. We need these kinds of fresh insights to jolt us into a new level of alertness.

Parodying life in humorous skits can make our real goals clearer when they can tend to get obscured by our sufferings. As the competition gets tougher and we work with more devotion, commitment, and dedication, our addiction that comes about from an old mystique about the nature of learning a performing art, intensifies our serious ideals of being a professional musician. When we reach a saturation point it is neccesary to blow off steam with the use of humor to gain some perspective.

To break the serious nature of our logical, analytical, "left brain," self, we can tap the resources of our intuitive, imaginative, "right brain," self. We can laugh when we get the image of our brain hemispheres as two different characters: the left-brain character square-shouldered and bossy, full of self-importance, and ready to analyze and direct each action logically with its store of verbal intelligence; and the right-brain character in a day-dream, intuitive and imaginative, full of wisdom but not too great with words, and not very practical. We could imagine the right-brain quietly getting a job done well if given the chance by one of our experiments. However, the left-brain character, momentarily tricked out of taking charge, pushes itself right back into the act and tries to dominate. This is an over-simplification of a complex process, but Ristad certainly gives us an image that is helpful.[71]

In finding ways to cope with the pressures of auditioning, we have seen that learning to use our creative resources to find humor can

---

[70]Eloise Ristad, *A Soprano on Her Head* (Utah: Real People Press, 1982) 13.
[71]Ibid. 37-42.

become a real advantage in not only gaining control, but also in enduring the audition procedure with enjoyment. In summary, humor helps us in overwhelming situations by:

giving us perspective;

taking our situation less seriously;

blowing off steam;

showing us new possibilities on how to view an event;

de-powering our perfectionistic attitudes;

helping us accept our predicament;

venting anger and frustrations;

giving us distance from our situation;

helping us find courage inside of ourselves; and

breaking tension.

DIET AND DRUGS

Coping with audition fears demands that we give our attentions over to finding the techniques which best help us feel in control. Because the body seems as if it were in revolt during stressful times, it is important to learn how not to aggravate those bodily symptoms that excite our system. For instance, enjoying cake and ice cream before an audition would elevate stress levels considerably, as the extra sugar charge one would feel may easily be misconstrued for nerves.

Robert Triplett (*Stage-fright*), says,

It is true that diet alone, just as relaxation techniques by themselves, cannot eliminate the stress of stagefright. Performance stress is more an attitude, and good diet cannot change our view of performance. Yet whereas certain foods of questionable value actually elevate stress levels, nutritious food can help us meet the stress that may already be present.[72]

---

[72]Triplett, loc. cit., 183.

Stress slows down digestion and makes the digestive tract particularly susceptible to alien elements. For this reason the system should not be taxed on the audition day with large meals or foods to which the body is unaccustomed. It is better to rely on a backlog of nutritious meals rather than attempt to cram in all the nutrients at the last minute. The body needs at least 12 to 14 days before dietary improvements can be effected. If stress levels are high, one should avoid eating anything but a healthful snack 3 or 4 hours before the event.[73]

SUGAR

A big slug of sugar can shock the pancreas into making too much insulin, which dramatically lowers blood sugar. This creates an emergency situation for the body and as SOS signal is sent to the adrenal glands, which respond by sending out the adrenalin to find more sugar. A low sugar-response can make one feel jittery, tired, hungry, and full all at the same time. On one hand, low blood sugar creates fatigue, sluggishness, and fuzzy thinking. On the other hand, the adrenalin response to meet the low-sugar emergency stimulates the body and thus creates a faster heartbeat, restless feelings of apprehension, and a state of insomnia. Symptoms of low blood sugar are:

depression;

anxiety;

irritability;

lack of concentration;

forgetfulness;

confusion;

headache;

body tremors; and
cold hands and feet.[74]

---

[73]Ibid. 192.
[74]Ibid. 185-86.

To help insure a proper sugar level, complex carbohydrates can help keep glucose levels balanced and are used when sugar is metabolized. These foods can help the body stay in balance:

brown rice;

whole wheat;

barley;

rye;

whole grain products;

soybeans;

mung beans;

peas;

lentils; and

other legumes.

Fruit juices are best when diluted by an equal portion of water to slow down the sugar absorption process. Better yet, the entire fruit should be consumed rather than just the juice.[75]

VITAMINS

VITAMIN B-COMPLEX. There seems to be an indirect connection between symptoms of a vitamin B shortage and various signs of stagefright. Symptoms include: tremors, loss of manual dexterity, lack of coordination, anxiety, depression, insomnia, forgetfulness, confusion, quick temper, and nervousness. Foods that are B-complex rich include:

whole grains;

legumes;

fresh vegetables; and

some milk products.

VITAMIN C, ASCORBIC ACID. Vitamin C is an important ingredient in helping decrease stress levels in several areas including mental

---

[75]Ibid. 187.

strain, physical overexertion, and body stress associated with diseases such as colds and flu. The most popular sources of vitamin C are:

citrus fruit;

fresh fruits;

most vegetables; and

calcium (aids proper absorption)

MINERALS. Calcium, magnesium, manganese, potassium, sodium, lithium, zinc, copper, chromium and chloride are all important to keep proper muscle fiber, nerve endings, brain tissue, and mood and emotion balance, as well as blood content. Good sources of minerals are:

calcium;

leafy vegetables;

mustard greens;

whole grains;

legumes;

tea;

fresh fruits;

apples;

bananas;

grapefruit;

broccoli;

spinach;

kelp;

oysters;

chard;

watercress;

tomatos;

pineapple;

fish; and

oats.[76]

LIQUIDS. Drink plenty of liquids, especially hard spring water, which is considered best for the body.[77]

When preparing for an audition follow these GUIDELINES FOR KEEPING SUGAR LEVELS AT A STABLE MAXIMUM (suggested by Robert Triplett):

1. Emphasize complex carbohydrates such as whole grains, most legumes, potatos, and bananas.

2. Reduce or eliminate simple starches and sugars such as white flour, honey, molasses, and white sugar.

3. Emphasize foods rich in vitamin B such as whole grains, legumes, lecithin, nutritional yeast, dark green leafy vegetables, and sour milk products.

4. Rely on whole fruits (except grapes) to satisfy a sweet tooth.

5. Avoid alcohol, nicotine, caffeine, and sugar in all forms. In many ways these are killers for a performer:

   A. All stimulate the adrenal glands.

   B. All confuse sugar metabolism and run the risk of creating a low-sugar response. Because they do so, all can potentially become addictive physiologically as well as psychologically.

   C. Caffeine found in coffee, tea, and chocolate destroys digestive enzymes.

   D. Cigarette smoke consumes vitamin C.

   E. Alcohol and sugar leach B vitamins from the system.[78]

---

[76]Ibid. 189-90.
[77]John McCamy, *Human Life Styling* (New York: Harper and Row, 1975) 93.
[78]Ibid. 194.

DRUGS

The use of medications is one of the most significant contributions of Western medicine to reduce a person's suffering. Many musicians use "underground" drugs to help them through a bad concert or audition. Used occasionally, psychologists and specialists in the field find certain drug usage is of benefit in helping one to cope with a lot of pressure. The trouble comes when these drugs are abused or become a crutch. If you find you need them or would like to try them, contact a physican, who will listen to your fears and write an appropriate prescription. One should proceed with caution when using them due to some side effects and possible addiction.

If you are considering using medication, R. Reid Wilson, author of the book *Don't Panic*, gives a few suggestions which will make your decision easier:

BEGIN BY OBTAINING AN ACCURATE DIAGNOSIS. Get a complete physical to see if there is a physical cause of your anxiety. If no physical diagnosis can be made, your physician should refer you to a licensed mental health professional who specializes in anxiety disorders for an evaluation.

THERE IS NO MAGIC PILL. The key to a successful cure lies in each individual's sense of his personal ability to face and overcome panic. All professional interventions should have but one purpose: to stabilize your belief that you are able to exert personal control over your body and your life.

BE WILLING TO TOLERATE SOME SIDE EFFECTS OF MEDICATIONS. Each medication can have side effects and you should familiarize yourself with them in the drug description below.

IF YOU DECIDE TO USE MEDICATION, GIVE IT A FAIR TRIAL. In order to evaluate the benefit of a medication, you must give it enough time to provide its therapeutic effect.

YOU WILL NOT REMAIN ON MEDICATION INDEFINITELY. Usually, a six-month to one-year drug treatment is sufficient.

YOU MUST TAPER OFF THESE MEDICATIONS GRADUALLY. Do not abruptly discontinue your daily dosage.

119

MEDICATIONS ARE OPTIONAL. You always have a choice regarding the use of medication. Do not let anyone persuade you that drugs are required in order to overcome your problems.[79]

Here is a listing of the major anxiety-reducing drugs available and some pertinent information regarding each:

TRICYCLIC ANTIDEPRESSANTS

Tricyclic antidepressants are traditionally used in the treament of severe depression or depression which occurs with anxiety. Of this family, IMIPRIMINE has been the focus of most of the research on the treatment of panic.

POSSIBLE BENEFITS. May reduce panic attacks and elevate a depressed mood.

DOSAGES RECOMMENDED BY INVESTIGATORS. The trial medication can begin with as little as 10 to 25 milligrams (mg) per day. If the patient adjusts to the side effects, the dosage is increased by 25 mg every two or more days until the preferred dosage is reached. The usual dosage is between 150 mg and 250 mg per day.

SIDE EFFECTS: Dry mouth, blurred vision, constipation, difficulty in urination, postural hypotension, and tachycardia (rapid heart beat). Sometimes these side effects will disappear with the passage of time or with a decrease in the dosage. Some people may experience side effects on dosages as low as 10 mg per day: jitteriness, irritation, unusual energy, and difficulty falling or staying asleep.

ALPRAZOLAM

Alprazolam (trade name XANAX) is a new medication in the benzodiazepine family, which includes anti-anxiety drugs. Other medications in this family, such as Valium and Tranxene, seem to have no benefit.

POSSIBLE EFFECTS. May reduce anticipatory anxiety and panic attacks; is rapid-acting and has few side effects.

DOSAGES RECOMMENDED BY INVESTIGATORS. Alprazolam is usually started at 0.25 mg or 0.5 mg, 3 times a day. If taken after

---

[79]R. Reid Wilson., *Don't Panic* (New York: Harper & Row, 1986).

meals, the side effects, such as drowsiness, are diminished and the therapeutic effects can last longer. This dosage may be increased by adding 0.5 mg to one of the three daily doses until a dose of 2 mg 3 times per day is reached. From that level, any additional increases are given at bedtime or applied equally during the day. The dosage range is from 2 to 6 mg per day.

POSSIBLE SIDE EFFECTS. Tiredness (sedation), unsteadiness of gait, slurring of speech, and, occasionally, headaches. Some patients may experience a depressed, irritable mood in the early weeks of the trial. Usually the side effects of alprazolam are not serious and will disappear with passage of time or with a lowering of the dosage.

MONOAMINE OXIDASE INHIBITORS
Monoamine oxidase inhibitors (MAO inhibitors) is the collective name for the drugs in the other major antidepressant family. NARDIL has been the MAO inhibitor most researched in regard to the treatment of panic.

POSSIBLE BENEFITS. May reduce panic attacks, elevate depressed mood, and increase confidence.

DIETARY RESTRICTIONS. The patient using an MAO inhibitor must be quite responsible, since this medication requires significant dietary restrictions. No cheese, red wine, beer, chocolate, yeast extracts, meats prepared with tenderizer, pickled herring, sour cream, yogurt, chicken livers, canned figs, raisins, soy sauce, bananas, avocados, fava beans, or lima beans are to be eaten while on this medication. These foods contain a substance called tyramine, which when combined with an MAO inhibitor can cause dangerously high blood pressure and severe headaches.

MEDICATION RESTRICTIONS. You should ALWAYS consult the prescribing physician prior to taking any additional medications. This especially includes over-the-counter cold medications (including nose drops or sprays), amphetamines, diet pills, tricyclic antidepressants, and certain antihistamines.

DOSAGES RECOMMENDED BY INVESTIGATORS. Each tablet of phenelzine is 15 mg. Dosage is 3 to 6 tablets per day, usually based on body weight.

POSSIBLE SIDE EFFECTS. Postural hypotension, difficulty sleeping, increased appetite, orgasmic dysfunction, drowsiness, dry mouth, and hypertensive crises.

PROPRANOLOL (INDERAL)

Propranolol (Inderal) belongs within the family of medication known as beta-adrenergic blocking agents, or "beta-blockers." It is traditionally used to treat high blood pressure, angina, certain heart conditions, and migraines.

POSSIBLE BENEFITS. May reduce some peripheral symptoms of anxiety, such as tachycardia and sweating, and general tension; can help control symptoms of stagefright and public-speaking fears; and has few side effects.

RESTRICTIONS ON USE. Propranolol should not be taken by patients with chronic lung disease, asthma, diabetes, and certain heart diseases, or by patients who are severely depressed.

DOSAGES RECOMMENDED BY INVESTIGATORS. Usually propranolol is taken 3 to 4 times per day for a total of 40 to 160 mg. The prescribing physician may determine dosage, in part, by monitoring the patient's resting heart rate. This medication can be used in combination with imiprimine or alprazolam.

POSSIBLE SIDE EFFECTS. Short-term memory loss, unusually slow pulse, lethargy, diarrhea, cold hands and feet, numbness and/or tingling of fingers or toes, dizziness or lightheadedness. If you have low blood-pressure, it is recommended you drink large quantities of water.

Other natural substances which have been found to relax a performer include certain teas such as chamomile and a combination of calcium and magnesium named Dolomite.

The use of drugs in controlling the symptoms of fear felt at an audition should be thought out carefully. The underground musician's drug," Inderal, is in widespread use today. However, one should use caution by understanding the side effects of a given drug and by realizing that an addiction to drugs may occur and that this may therefore not be the ideal approach to a problem of stagefright.

Chapter IV

⋘ↁↄ⋙

SUCCESSFUL ATTITUDES AND OUTLOOKS FOR AUDITIONING

SITUATIONAL FOCUS

Before entering an audition, it is a good idea to be mentally prepared with a healthy attitude and realistic expectations. Whether a person wins or loses an audition should not affect him before the actual performance. Instead it is a good idea to build up confidence, view the competition in a pleasant way, trust yourself and your abilities, and find your strength in your own individuality.

In Maxwell Maltz's book, *Psycho-Cybernetics*, there are some suggestions for keeping a good attitude in situations. They include:

1. GLANCE AT NEGATIVES, BUT FOCUS ON POSITIVES. A negative signal does not mean you are no good, but you should keep your attention on your goal.

2. CRISIS MEANS DECISIVENESS OR POINT OF DECISION. Think about what you want to happen and maintain an aggressive attitude by reacting aggressively.[1]

3. THINK IN TERMS OF END RESULTS. Trust yourself to supply the means whereby it is fulfilled.

4. THINK IN TERMS OF A PRESENT POSSIBILITY. This activates your creative mechanisms.[2]

5. FEELING LIKE A FAILURE IS NOT A SURE SIGN THAT YOU ARE. You will perform badly if you react to your feelings and what attitude you take toward them. If you listen to them, obey them, and take counsel of them, your confidence will be shaken.

[1]Maxwell Maltz, *Psycho- Cybernetics* (New York: Prentice-Hall, Inc. 1980) 215.
[2]Ibid. 223.

6. REACTIVATING MEMORIES OF PAST FAILURES RATHER THAN POSITIVE ONES IS UNDERESTIMATING YOUR ABILITIES.[3]

7. LET YOUR CREATIVITY WORK FOR YOU. Learn to trust it and do not jam it by becoming too concerned or too anxious.[4]

8. DEVELOP EMOTIONAL TOUGHNESS AND EGO-SECURITY TO PROTECT YOU FROM REAL AND FANCIED EGO-THREATS. Having too thin and too sensitive a "skin" will protect us from minor threats.[5] Develop a healthy self-image that is not threatened by conflict.

9. BE SELF-RELIANT AND RESPONSIBLE FOR YOURSELF. Having sufficient self-reliance will provide ego-security. Be more giving and you will find you will have more support.

10. RELAXATION CUSHIONS EMOTIONAL BLOWS. Try to keep your muscles perfectly relaxed during times of stress.[6]

11. IF YOU CANNOT IGNORE A BAD RESPONSE, DELAY IT. Try to put off worry until tomorrow if you feel tension overwhelming you in the present.

12. BUILD A QUIET ROOM IN YOUR MIND. Meditation can calm and focus your mind in times of stress.[7]

13. LEARN TO PRACTICE WITHOUT PRESSURE. Try to develop a new response to stress.

14. CULTIVATE FAITH AND COURAGE. Define yourself by picturing the best possible outcome and mentally accept and digest these gradual doses of optimism and faith.[8]

15. ACCEPT NEGATIVE FEELINGS AS A CHALLENGE. Try to react aggressivly and positively to your negative feelings and it will arouse more power and more ability in you.[9]

[3]Ibid 236.
[4]Ibid. 29.
[5]Ibid. 154.
[6]Ibid. 156.
[7]Ibid. 192.
[8]Ibid. 235.
[9]Ibid. 237.

16. DO NOT MISTAKE EXCITEMENT FOR FEAR. Being excited or nervous before a performance is determined by how you react to it. Try to direct your energy toward your goal and use it as additional strength.[10]

Other authors add the following suggestions:

17. ALL YOU CAN CONTROL IS THE INPUT YOU PROVIDE IN A SITUATION. You can pride yourself on good consistent work regardless of the outcome.[11].

18. SURRENDER TO THE OUTCOME OF AN EVENT WITHOUT ATTACHMENT TO THE RESULT. Focus on the spirit behind the action rather than the form of the action itself.[12]

19. THROW YOURSELF WITHOUT RESTRAINT INTO THE POSSIBILITIES OF THE MOMENT. Surrender your conscious expectations and fears and bring as much creativity to an event as you can.[13]

20. DESIRE TO PROVIDE THE SERVICE THAT IS REQUIRED. The difference between attitude and action is going through the motions and wanting to provide service.[14]

21. WE FEAR THE UNFAMILIAR. To conquer our apprehensions we need to do the thing we are afraid of, and then repeat the process until the experience is as familiar as an old friend.[15]

22. GETTING UP THE COURAGE TO GO THERE IS THE HARDEST STEP. When you do the things you fear, you begin to whittle that fear down to a size you can handle.[16]

23. DON'T COMPARE YOURSELF WITH OTHERS. This will get you into a good-bad, winner-loser syndrome.[17]

---

[10]Ibid. 217.

[11]David D. Burns, M.D., *Feeling Good* (New York: William Morrow and Co., Inc., 1980) 84.

[12]Elizabeth Brenner, *Winning by Letting Go* (San Diego: Harcourt Brace Jovanovich, 1985) 104.

[13]Ibid. 159.

[14]Ibid. 173.

[15]Marty Baxter, *Over-Come Stage Fright* (New York: Bradley Publications, 1982) 14.

[16]Ibid. 23.

[17]Ibid. 27.

24. TURN STRESS TO CREATIVE ADVANTAGE. A goal for all
performers is to realize that stress is part of the job and to
learn how to manage it.

When approaching an audition, it is important to have a clear and
focused state of mind. A clear level of consciousness can bring about
healthy attitudes and peace of mind, while a confused thought system
can bring insecurity and anxiety. In her book, *Understanding*, Jane
Nelson cites this graphic representation of the states of mind we
experience when we are thinking from a clear, focused consciousness
and when we are thinking from our programmed, automatic thought
system.

CLEAR CHANNEL	THOUGHT SYSTEM
(high level consciousness)	(low level consciousness)
Security	Insecurity
Love	Judgment
Happiness	Coping
Compassion	Expectations
Satisfaction	Dissatisfaction
Understanding	Assumptions
Insight	Stress
Realization	Rules (shoulds/shouldn'ts)
Forgiveness	Right vs. wrong
Gratitude	Blame
Sense of humor	Anger
Common sense	Interpretations
Wisdom	Anxiety
Inspiration	Proving ego
Peace of mind	Inadequacy
The beauty of now	Past or future oriented
Natural positive feelings	Positive thinking[18]

Having a healthy attitude going into an audition can give us power
and optimism. Using the resources we have within us can make the
experience a positive one and not a dreadful battle. The next four
sections will show specific ways of building confidence, seeing the

---

[18]Jane Nelson, *Understanding* (California: Sunrise Press, 1986) 22.

event with new insights, trusting one's ability, and gaining power by realizing one's strong points.

BUILDING CONFIDENCE

Learning to develop a healthy perspective towards auditioning takes a firm base of self-confidence. This confidence comes from an honest self-assurance when we give up our protective devices and willfully enter a pressure-laden situation. By moving through our fears we emerge seeing new qualities on the other side.

This confidence is not to be confused with blind confidence. This false confidence is a reward promised, but never delivered. When we try to summon up the strength to fight our fears, we seek a protector who can push the "magic button" and give us the confidence we need to face the audition. Blind confidence seems "out there" just beyond our grasp, if we only knew where to locate it. The answer to fear is not in blind-confidence, but in the courage to give in to the fear.[19]

There are three major causes for low self-confidence:

1. SELF-DEFEATING CONCEPTS, BELIEFS AND VALUES.

2. FALSE AND DISTORTED CONCEPTS ABOUT OURSELVES GIVEN TO US BY TEACHERS, PARENTS, AND OTHER OUTSIDE INFLUENCES.

3. NEGATIVE CONDITIONING WHICH EMPHASIZES FEELINGS OF GUILT AND UNWORTHINESS.[20]

Low self-esteem has many different manifestations. They all can be described as the means and habits we develop in order to escape the demands of everyday living as well as the competition of auditions. They are simply alibis which permit us to temporarily avoid facing up to personal reality. The degree to which we feel insecure is in direct ratio to our fear of having to justify who and what we are. The person

[19]Robert Triplett, *Stage-fright: Letting It Work For You* (Chicago: Nelson-Hall, 1983) 62-63.
[20]Robert Anthony, *Total Self-Confidence* (San Diego: Berkley Publishing Corporation, 1979) 33.

with low self-confidence uses his alibi to cover up inadequacies he does not want others to see.[21]

Finding our self-confidence during stressful times is sometimes very difficult. When fear and worry seem to overtake our minds, it confuses us and it's hard to think clearly. It is at times like these that we must talk back to the phobic images invading our consciousness. Below is a listing of coping strategies which can help build our self-confidence and empower our body, mind, and spirit.

1. REALIZE THAT YOU CREATE YOUR LIFE. You have the power to change any aspect of your life.

2. FULFILL YOUR OWN NEEDS FIRST. Do not worry about the whole world: if you do, it will overwhelm you. Please yourself, do something for you, and the rest will fall into place.

3. TRY TO VIEW LIFE WITHOUT YOUR OWN PERSONAL "MISTAKEN CERTAINTIES." Do not assume that you know how life is by your own personal perspective. A lot of your own beliefs are based on a limited viewpoint. Be aware of "what is" and accept reality.

4. FIND YOUR SOLID FOUNDATION OF SELF-RELIANCE. A self-confident personality allows you to stand on your own two feet and to believe that you can handle problems that come up. Listen to your own cue from what you are rather than listening to something outside of you.

5. DO NOT COMPARE YOURSELF TO OTHERS. Comparison is a sign of low self-esteem and a fear that others are above you.

6. COMPETITION KILLS CREATIVITY. You were put on this earth to create, not compete. Thinking in terms of being "better than" the next person will conspire against you and dampen your spirit. Think in terms of the reward being found in the doing and not in the end result. Strive for excellence in your own life rather than trying to be "better than" someone else.

7. DO NOT SEEK THE APPROVAL OF OTHERS. Praise-seeking implies that you must constantly prove your worth and try to be or do "better than" someone else. It is a game you can never win. The

[21]Ibid. 37.

most destructive power of praise lies in its ability to make you identify with your actions and labels you as "good" or "bad." Try to stop placing others above you.

8. ACCEPT YOURSELF AS YOU ARE. You are a truly unique and worthy individual who does not have to impress others with achievements or material possessions.

9. RECOGNIZE THAT YOUR ACTIONS ARE BUT THE MEANS YOU CHOOSE TO FULFILL YOUR DOMINANT NEEDS. Your actions do not really describe who you are; they are only descriptions of the things you do. By identifying with your actions you are falsely perceiving the truth about yourself. You are judging, limiting, and rejecting yourself without justification. You are not your actions. They may be wise or unwise, but again, they do not classify you as "good" or "bad.

10. WATCH YOUR NEED FOR ATTENTION AND APPROVAL. People with low self-esteem have compulsive needs as they are not able to recognize and appreciate themselves as worthy, adequate individuals of importance.

11. NOTICE IF YOU HAVE AN AGGRESSIVE NEED TO WIN. If you have an obsessive need to win or be right all the time, you are suffering from a desperate need to prove yourself. The motivation is always to receive acceptance and approval, trying to be "better than" someone else.

12. INDECISION AND PROCRASTINATION COME FROM A FEAR OF MAKING MISTAKES. Fearing that you will not live up to the expectations of others causes delays in decisions.

13. SELF-PITY RESULTS FROM THE INABILITY TO TAKE CHARGE OF OUR LIFE. Allowing yourself to be at the mercy of people, circumstances, and conditions shows a leaning, dependent personality that likes attention and sympathy.

14. REALIZE THAT YOU ALWAYS DO YOUR BEST. You can never do better than you are doing at this moment because you are limited by your present level of awareness. Even if your best is faulty, to know better is not sufficient to do better. You will only "do better" when your level of awareness is expanded.

15. ACCEPT REALITY. You can only be happy and at peace with yourself to the degree that you accept reality as it is in the present frame of reference within which you are operating. When you do, you will no longer be vulnerable to the adverse opinions of others.

16. RECOGNIZE THAT NO OTHER ACTION IS POSSIBLE AT THE TIME. Every action is based on your present level of awareness. Do not resist your own view of what is.

17. STOP ALL VALUE-JUDGING. Do not impose what you have decided is "right" or "wrong" on yourself as it will make you resentful and angry. Realize that everyone must inevitably do what they have to, whether it is correct or not.

18. UNDERSTAND YOUR MOTIVATION FOR WHAT YOU ARE DOING. Describe your attitude when you would rather do one thing or another. Fulfill your need to feel good.

19. RECOGNIZE SELF-IMPOSED GUILT. Realize that the past cannot be changed and try to learn from it.

20. TRUST YOUR CREATIVE SELF. Finding that part of yourself will give you the information you need to head in the right direction.

21. FIND OUT WHAT IT IS THAT YOU DESIRE. Creative powers channel themselves through that which we desire. Trust your intuition to point out what you want.

22. USE YOUR IMAGINATION TO CREATE MEANINGFUL IMAGES AND PICTURES. Use your creative mind to plant the seeds of what you want to grow in situations where you see few or no options.

23. NO MATTER WHAT HAPPENS, IF YOUR INTENTION WAS GOOD, THEN IT CAN BE SEEN AS A VICTORY. Accepting failure and success is easier if your beliefs and convictions are true to yourself.

24. TRY TO EVOKE A GOOD FEELING OR EMOTION. This can help create a mood of self-confidence when you are not in the state of mind you wish to be in.

25. DETACH YOURSELF FROM THE END RESULT. Try to picture the results you want, yet stay neutral to the reality of the moment.

26. DESIGN A CREATIVE PLAN. This will give you purpose and direction as well as conviction.

27. SET GOALS IN THE SIX MAJOR AREAS OF YOUR LIFE. Give direction to your career, financial goals, physical health, mental knowledge, family goals, and spiritual needs.

28. TRY TO GAIN PERSPECTIVE. Learn to relax now, in the present, with no fear or concern about what is going to happen in the future.

29. MAKE FRIENDS WITH FAILURE. Failure is a tool you can use to learn to grow if you are persistent and if you do not let your need for approval dampen your spirit.

30. USE MEDITATION TO FOCUS AND RELAX. Meditation can increase oxygen consumption, decrease lactic acid in the blood, slow the heart rate, create deep rest, stabilize the nervous system, speed up reaction time, increase the intelligence rate, improve the self-image, and improve performance.

31. MANAGE YOURSELF. Take control over your life by doing the things you need to do.

32. LEARN TO ACCEPT CHANGE. It is a rule of the universe that everything changes, so we must learn to accept and look forward to it. Stop fighting changes and see what you can do to improve things. Think of the benefits you will receive as you create changes for the better.

33. TAKE CONSTRUCTIVE ACTION. Positive thinking allows you to build on your strengths while overcoming your weaknesses and to tolerate your limitations.

34. USE THESE POSITIVE STATEMENTS TO RELEASE YOUR CREATIVE POWER AND INCREASE YOUR CONFIDENCE:

    A. At this moment I am prepared and equipped to accept my limitless potential.

    B. My thinking, vision, and anticipation are in the now.

C. I am creative in my approach to myself and know that the creative being that I am knows how to create from within me.

D. I am mentally and emotionally dedicated to my own good and to the good of others. I live in a friendly universe which responds to my healthy desires and brings them to pass.

E. I accept the fact that I am a unique individual with a place to occupy and a special purpose to fulfill.

F. I will expand my awareness by getting rid of "mistaken certainties" which are preventing me from releasing my unlimited potential.

G. I will release my unlimited potential by choosing a goal and making a plan for myself.

H. I will look within to my power to solve problems and make life as I wish it to be.

I. I will visualize and affirm whatever it is that I want to be, do, or have in my life experience.

J. I will give my dominant thoughts to success, not failure.

K. I will get rid of dependency, worry and fear by cultivating self-reliance, love, imagination, enthusiasm, a sense of humor, and the ability to communicate.

L. I will meditate to achieve peace, power, and fulfillment.

M. I am endowed with the ability to choose and the potential power to accomplish anything I desire.

In learning to develop self-confidence, it is important to be able to tap into the many resources which are available to us. These resources include accepting reality as it is, gaining perspective, trusting ourselves and many other imaginative techniques which can help us realize our potential.

REFRAMING OLD OUTLOOKS

When we view an event from a different perspective than we did previously, we see it with new qualities and in a different light. When reframing a situation, such as an audition, we want to be able to say, "Hey, how else can I do this?" We want to find alternative ways to function more effectively and enjoy those situations that are paved with peril.

When we think of taking an audition, we suddenly get bombarded with images of fear, frustration, and hopelessness. Instead of looking for what is wrong and fixing it, we can take the approach of thinking of ways to enrich our lives: "What would be fun or interesting to do?" "What new capacities or abilities could I invent for myself?" or "How can I make things really fantastic?"[22]

One of the advantages of being human is that we can choose to think one thing or another. If you choose to find ways in which to enjoy your life more, one kind of thinking will aid you, while another will sabotage it.[23]

In their book, *Frogs into Princes*, Richard Bandler and John Grinder describe in detail the process of reframing. Using this technique, it is possible to change the way you feel and think about auditions.

1. IDENTIFY THE PATTERN OR BEHAVIOR TO BE CHANGED. The first step is to name the things you wish to stop doing, such as worrying too much, or focusing on the difficult passages in the music.

2. ESTABLISH COMMUNICATION WITH THE PART RESPONSIBLE FOR THE PATTERN. Ask yourself:

   A. "Will the part of me that runs pattern X communicate with me in consciousness?"

   B. Establish the "yes-no" meaning of the signal/feeling received. During a time of quiet reflection, address yourself to that area which seems identified with the problem and ask if it will co-operate with you to establish an open line of communication.

3. DISTINGUISH BETWEEN THE BEHAVIOR, PATTERN X, AND THE INTENTION OF THE PART THAT IS RESPONSIBLE FOR THE BEHAVIOR. Ask:

[22]Richard Bandler, *Frogs into Princes* (Utah: Real People Press, 1979) 190.
[23]Albert Ellis, *A New Guide to Rational Living* (New Jersey: Prentice-Hall, 1975) 33.

A. "Would you be willing to let me know in consciousness what you are trying to do for me by pattern X?"

B. If you get a "yes" response, ask the part to go ahead and communicate its intention.

C. Is that intention acceptable to consciousness? The specific method being used to cause you trouble has to be recognized as unacceptable to you. You may not like the way that it goes about accomplishing pattern X, (that unwanted behavior), but you do see that the INTENTION is something you want to have. This congruency between the intention of the subconscious part and the APPRECIATION of the conscious is important at this time, although if no conscious answer appears, it will not hurt this technique.

D. CREATE NEW ALTERNATIVE BEHAVIORS TO SATISFY THE INTENTION. At the unconscious level, the part that runs pattern X communicates its intention to the creative part and selects from the alternatives generated by the creative part. Each time it selects an alternative it gives the "yes" signal. Therefore, finding more successful ways in accomplishing what it is that you want can be gotten from your creative self. Creating better ways to get to that outcome will help you find a more effective way to cope with the problems at an audition.

E. ASK THAT PART, "ARE YOU WILLING TO TAKE RESPONSIBILITY FOR GENERATING THREE NEW ALTERNATIVES IN THE APPROPRIATE CONTEXT?" In this step we want to make sure that those choices actually occur in our behavior.

F. ECOLOGICAL CHECK. "IS THERE ANY OTHER PART OF ME THAT OBJECTS TO THE THREE NEW ALTERNATIVES?" If there is a "yes" response, recycle to step two.[24]

In using this reframing strategy, you can prevent a certain type of behavior from happening and change the behavior which is disturbing your performance. Understanding what gain is derived from your problems will help you arrive at new and more useful ways in which to

---

[24]Bandler, loc. cit. 160.

cope. Using this technique on a specific fear would look something like this:

1. I want to stop my hands from shaking.

2. Will the part of me that is making my hands shake speak to me? (yes or no)

3. I want to understand what my behavior of shaky hands will do for me. Is it to protect me? Is my adrenalin being absorbed in that part of my body so that another part will not get out of control? Is it doing something on my behalf as a total person? (Knowing that your problem is in your best interest, or even just feeling it, is good enough to proceed.)

4. Are there some other ways to react to auditions instead of with shaky hands? Perhaps I can notice the rhythm more by tapping my foot, let my hands shake and pretend that they are clapping at my performance or rest my fingers on the keys or fingerboard so my reflexes will be all that much quicker.

5. Ask myself if I am willing to do these things when I am at an audition.

6. Ask if there is any part of me that objects to the new ways of coping.

Albert Ellis describes other ways in which to view a situation:

1. YOU CAN REFUSE TO RATE YOURSELF. Only your acts get rated; not "you."

2. DISCRIMINATE INAPPROPRIATE FROM APPROPRIATE EMOTIONS. Clearly define what you choose as your values and decide which feelings are useful.

3. USE IMAGINATIVE TECHNIQUES. Positive imagery can get you in touch with emotions and thoughts that will bring on confidence and authority.[25]

Robert Anthony recommends the following to help change certain behaviors:

[25]Ellis, loc. cit. 202-13.

1. Recognize those habits you want to change.

2. What positive attitude will you develop to replace them?

3. What actions will you take to replace your negative habit?

4. What is the easiest and most logical way to do this?

5. Visualize yourself as already having succeeded in changing your habit. See yourself enjoying the benefits of your new positive habit.

6. Use positive coping statements to affirm your visualization.

7. Observe your actions and make a note of each time you fail to do what you promised. Make non-judgmental observations and allow yourself to make any necessary corrections.

8. Learn to accept change and look forward to it, rather than fighting it.[26]

In his article, "Coping with Stage Fright," Michael Colgrass tells of his method of reframing a fearful situation in Carnegie Hall.

My own method of allaying stagefright is through changing any preconceived notions I might have about what's scaring me. Take for example Carnegie Hall. It's the TRADITION of that hall that's forboding, not the actual audience or performing conditions. I was recently asked to give a casual talk there to the audience before the performance of one of my orchestral pieces. It was an important occasion with a major orchestra, and I was nervous about it. The day of the concert was a madhouse and I got little rest or proper food (typical of a performer's life on the road), so when concert time came I was edgy and tired. My piece was last on the program. At intermission I went back to the green room (the artist's lounge named for its soothing color), took off my jacket, shoes, cuff links, and tie and stood on my head and wiggled my toes, which made me giggle. Then I did some mime exercises, stretching my hands and making funny faces. By now the second half of the concert had started and the orchestra was playing a Haydn symphony; which I could hear through the speaker system, so I danced to the minuet and thought to myself, "I wonder what the audience would think if they could see me now." Then I

---

[26]Anthony, loc. cit., 58-62.

washed my face, put myself together and went downstairs and stood in the wings. I felt energetic and ready, but not nervous, and the talk went well.

The exercise had circulated my blood and awakened me, but, more importantly, I had changed my image of Carnegie Hall. In this most venerable of concert halls you are supposed to be dignified, sophisticated and scared. You don't frolic around the green room with half your clothes off, giggling like a kid. Almost without knowing it, I had broken old associations with that hall and made new ones: to this day when I think of Carnegie Hall I see myself dancing backstage to a Haydn symphony.[27]

Another reframing technique that Michael Colgrass uses to help alleviate problems in performing is to split yourself into three parts so you are able to change your outlook on the situation.

1. Recall the feeling of a situation that was unpleasant for you. Then recall the time and place as best as you can–the sounds, the colors, the objects and don't worry about reliving that b-a-d feeling.

   Now the fun begins. Whatever was happening at that unpleasant time, run it through your mind again, but this time double-speed the action! Then triple-speed! Then quadruple-speed! Now run the action backwards, in slow motion! (I know it seems impossible, but do it anyway.)

2. Now watch (and listen) to that old situation from outside as if you were seeing yourself on TV. Take your time and watch the whole action carefully in the role as part one.

3. Now watch yourself in the role of part two watching yourself. Notice how much you're enjoying it when you are twice removed from the action.[28]

Another imaginative technique Michael Colgrass uses is to practice making pictures in his head. He suggests putting two imaginary screens up in front of your eyes, one with a pleasant memory picture

[27]Micheal Colgrass, Coping With Stage Fright (*Music Magazine*: November /December, 1981) 38.
[28]Michael Colgrass You should See Yourself (*Jam Magazine* : December 1983) 12.

and another with an unpleasant picture. Playing with imaginary dials on the screen, experiment with making the pictures brighter or darker, bigger or smaller, closer or more distant, and notice how your feelings change. Finish by leaving the dials on the setting you like.[29]

Having the goal of making auditioning as pleasant as possible, we can invent new ways to perceive those things which trouble us. Believing that we are not doomed to suffer our usual audition symptoms, we can gain strength in knowing that many options are available for use as tools for enjoyment.

TRUST

The moment a performer starts his walk into the audition room is the moment when insecurity feels the most real. Feelings of vulnerability and fear fill one's body and mind. It is during these moments that the strength to go on is needed most. This strength can be found in trust. A concrete trust in yourself as well as in your preparation is necessary for confidence to take over.

Trust is based on careful preparation–that by which we have expended every effort to consider each angle as it relates to a performance. After this is done, we can stop and rest, and then give in to faith. That is to say, we give up control and open ourselves to the energy of our natural talents. When we are ready to receive its power, it will be revealed and the "magic" moments will be ours to experience.[30]

Having a sense of clarified trust can restore a person's sense of well-being. Trust in oneself can bring fulfillment by the joyful discoveries made in our music-making AND in our selves.[31] Building self-confidence takes a recognition of our own true worth. How we feel about ourselves determines how we respond to life and its problems. If we develop a way to accept our way of being we automatically feel better about ourselves and are able to trust our talents, commitments, and risks.

[29]Ibid. 12.
[30]Triplett, loc. cit., 103.
[31]Ibid. 111.

In learning to trust ourselves, Barry Green cites three categories of obstacles which must be overcome.

1. PROBLEMS WITH SELF-IMAGE
   A. Are you concerned about the respect your peers feel for you?
   B. Are you concerned about what the audience will think of your playing?
   C. Are you worried you will be a failure?

2. DOUBTING YOUR CONTROL OF THE SITUATION
   A. Do you feel stuck with a "flat" or "ridgid" interpretation?

3. DOUBTING YOUR ABILITIES to loosen up and play creatively?
   A. Are you worried you just "don't have it" musically?
   B. Do you suffer from performance anxiety?
   C. Are you doubtful of your capacity to perform under pressure?[32]

Being you is the best thing you have; who you are, what you are, how you think, and the unique individuality that is you. You have the right to be everything that you are; to have all your feelings, and to express them. When you begin to accept that, you are on the road to trusting yourself. By knowing who you are, and by finding your real feelings, you then have the bricks to make your firm foundation as an artist.[33]

When doubts creep in, little voices keep saying, "It's going to sound phony; I'm not ready! I don't believe it; I don't feel what I want to feel;" and so on. Commentary short-circuits you from being in the moment and expressing what you feel. Trust is the antidote to the fear these voices bring.[34]

Here are some suggestions for learning how to trust yourself:

[32]Barry Green, *The Inner Game of Music* (New York: Anchor Press, 1986)
[33]Eric Morris, *Being and Doing* (California. Spelling Publications, 1981) 4.
[34]Ibid. 60.

1. BE YOURSELF, NO MATTER WHAT YOU THINK THE PEOPLE AROUND YOU EXPECT.

2. KNOW THE LOGIC AND MEANING OF THE MUSIC AND TRUST YOURSELF TO EXPRESS THE LINE IN TERMS OF WHAT YOU REALLY FEEL.

3. FLOW WITH THE MOMENT TO MOMENT IMPULSE AND NOT WITH WHAT YOU THINK IS ACCEPTABLE AUDITION BEHAVIOR.

4. TAKE SOME CHANCES THAT MAY MAKE YOU LOOK FOOLISH (BECAUSE YOU ARE LEAVING YOURSELF OPEN TO RIDICULE AS YOU ARE BEING WHAT YOU FEEL).

5. HAVE THE COURAGE TO REACH FOR YOUR OWN AUTHENTICITY.

6. BE WILLING TO HAVE SOME FAILURES AND TO TRY SOME MORE.[35]

7. KNOW THAT THERE IS MUSIC INSIDE OF YOU.

8. BE AT ONE WITH THE MUSIC THROUGH RELAXED CONCENTRATION.

9. DO NOT BE CONCERNED WITH WHAT THE AUDIENCE WILL THINK OF YOUR PLAYING.

10. TO FEEL IN CONTROL TRY TO LOOSEN UP AND TAKE RISKS.

11. PUT YOUR ATTENTION ON TRUSTING YOURSELF RATHER THAN YOUR AWARENESS AND WILL-POWER.

12. GIVE YOURSELF OVER TO THE CHARACTER AND EMOTIONS OF THE MUSIC.

13. LET THE CHARACTER OF THE MUSIC "SPEAK" THROUGH YOU.

14. EXPRESS THE QUALITIES OF THE MUSIC RATHER THAN EXHIBITING YOUR OWN PERSONALITY.

15. ACCEPT YOUR ROLE AS INTERPRETER AND YOU CAN CEASE TO BE SO WORRIED ABOUT HOW YOU APPEAR TO OTHERS.

---

[35]Morris, Ibid. 60.

16. OUR CONTROL IS BEST WHEN WE ARE LEAST AWARE OF IT.

17. EXAMINE THE CONSEQUENCES OF SUCCESS AND FAILURE AND THINK ABOUT YOUR PURPOSE AS A MUSICIAN.

18. TRY TO ROLE PLAY AND PRETEND YOU ARE SOMEONE YOU RESPECT.

19. BECOME THE MUSIC AND PERFORM WITHOUT SELF-CONSCIOUSNESS.[36]

20. SELF-ASSURANCE CONSISTS OF TRANQUIL COMMENDATION, FOCUSED BELIEF AND COURAGEOUS RISKING.[37]

21. TO TRUST OUR ABILITIES TAKES ACTIVATING A HIGHER ESSENCE DEEP WITHIN US THAT SEEKS MEANING, UNDERSTANDING AND PURPOSE.

22. TRUST THAT THERE DWELLS SOMEWHERE IN US A PRESENCE WISER THAN OUR ORDINARY AWARENESS.

23. CONSIDER THE BEAUTY YOU COMMUNICATE.

24. KNOW WHO YOU ARE.

25. TRUST IN YOUR PURPOSE.[38]

26. HOPE FOR AND EXPECT THE BEST.

27. THE MORE CONFIDENT YOU FEEL, THE MORE POWER YOU WILL HAVE.

28. GIVE YOURSELF PERMISSION TO FEEL SAFE.

29. SUPPORT YOUR OWN EFFORTS.

30. POINT OUT YOUR SUCCESSES AND USE THAT FEELING TO EMPOWER YOU.

31. LOOK AROUND YOU FOR SUPPORT.

32. ASK YOUR CRITICAL MIND TO QUIET DOWN AND TRUST YOUR INSTINCTS.[39]

[36]Green, loc. cit., 79-90.
[37] Triplett, loc. cit., 110.
[38]Ibid. 101-04.
[39]R. Reid Wilson, *Don't Panic* (New York: Harper and Row, 1986) 197, 262.

33. REMIND YOURSELF OF YOUR FREEDOMS AND CHOICES.

34. GIVE YOURSELF PERMISSION TO FEEL SAFE.

35. SUPPORT ALL YOUR EFFORTS.

36. INVITE YOURSELF TO FEEL CONFIDENT.

37. EXPECT A POSITIVE OUTCOME.

38. POINT OUT YOUR SUCCESSES.

39. LOOK AROUND FOR SUPPORT.

40. BELIEVE THAT YOU CAN CHANGE.

41. KNOW THAT THERE IS ALWAYS MORE THAN ONE OPTION IN DECISIONS.

42. FOCUS MORE ON SOLUTIONS THAN ON PROBLEMS.[40]

43. LEARN TO TRUST YOUR BODY AND LET YOUR MUSCLES RELAX.

44. FEEL GREATER SUPPORT IN YOUR BODY AND LEARN TO PERCEIVE MORE CONTROL OVER IT.[41]

CONCLUSION: INDIVIDUALITY

The topic of individuality was saved for the last because it is this characteristic which seems to be the most important ingredient in becoming a creative artist. Its absence, then, will make it difficult for one to survive in the competitive music world. Fortunately, we are all born into this world with a great amount of individuality. . . it is an appreciation for, and a conscious desire for the development of, this personality trait which gives us that extra charisma required to become one of the "greats."

At an audition, much of the power needed for a quality performance is found in the amount of confidence displayed by an individual. Knowing what is unique to ourselves, what makes us

[40]Ibid. 197
[41]Ibid. 232.

different and special, can give us a clear goal and purpose. Accepting who and what we are can lead us to appreciate our individuality.

It is hard to realize that there is only one person like us, and that person is ourself. We can have good feelings knowing that other people are variations of us, each having qualities that are a little bit different, yet just not the same. Discovering the ways of other people's lives can help us to grow and expand from our present life-position.[42]

We are our fears, our nutrition, our exercise, our expectations, our interpretations, our likes and dislikes, what people are telling us from the outside, and our faith in being able to grow. As students of life, we are balancing out our needs with our responsibilities with our wishes. We are constantly making decisions; in every situation we balance our losses and gains.[43]

Virginia Satir, in her book, *Your Many Faces,* speaks of how we experience our feelings. She says that our feelings are capable of both depleting and providing energy.

1. ENERGY PROVIDERS
   Hopefulness
   Helpfulness
   Powerfulness
   New Possibilities
   Change
   Choice

2. ENERGY DEPLETERS
   Hopelessness
   Helplessness
   Powerlessness
   No Possibility
   No Change
   No Choice[44]

---

[42]Virginia Satir, *Your Many Faces* (California: Celestial Arts, 1978) 96-98.
[43]Ibid. 108.
[44]Ibid. 23.

This list is very valuable to a performer, as he can use the "Energy Providers" as a power source to tap into when preparing for a performance or an audition. Finding the new possibilities in a piece of music, being hopeful that we can execute it, using the help given to us by our teacher or friends, changing certain elements to make it work, and choosing other influences, can help empower us and spur us on to a better display of our abilities.

Trusting who we are can give us a secure performance, in that we are able to clarify what is important to us. Knowing this we can then communicate the deeper message of emotional security and artistic conviction. Trusting defines our territory, and describes that which is our own.[45] By setting our territorial limits, we are defining our self, what we like, and what we cannot tolerate. If we know our self, we can have a sense of purpose and a knowledge of what we are intended to be.[46]

"A psychologically healthy man . . . bases his self-esteem on his rationality: on his dedication to knowing what is true and what is right in fact and in reality, and on acting consistently with his knowledge."[47] A person must think, judge, and choose what he thinks is important, before he has a distinct identity and can feel worthy of enjoying his values and life.[48] One's sense of value can enable him to view life as either an adventure or a frustration; as beautiful or senseless. He can be eager and self-confident or self-loathing and embittered. Therefore, the way in which a man views himself colors his world.[49]

Believing in our self gives us the strength to stand up in front of an audition committee and put our best foot forward. An inner conviction of the beliefs we are putting out is what is so important to a performer. Executing his creative insights is the goal of every musician, as he seeks to fulfill the concept waiting to be materialized.

[45], William Pietsch, *Human Be-ing* (New York: Signet Books, 1975) 78, 150.
[46]Ibid. 53.
[47]Nathaniel Branden, *The Psychology of Self-Esteem* (New York: Bantam Books, 1981) 187.
[48]Ibid. 238.
[49]Branden, loc. cit. 216.

Below is a listing, from various sources, of those qualities which are important in helping us be in contact with our individuality and our basic beliefs that make us what we are.

1. ENJOYMENT. When we discover what gives us pleasure and what we enjoy, we can derive what it is that gives us meaning.

2. CREATIVITY. Knowing what inspires us can help us be in touch with those forces that keep our interest.

3. JOY. Knowing what we love can give us warmth and feelings of great emotional pleasure.

4. KNOWLEDGE AND TRUTH. We can grow and expand as individuals when we gain new insights to our already gained knowlege.

5. SPIRITUALITY AND OUR HIGHER SELF. When we are able to touch that part of ourselves that is our soul, we can experience a great truth about ourself in relation to the universe.

6. HEALTHY GOALS. Once we have planned our own unique future, we will gain motivation for fulfilling our hopes and desires.

7. VALUES. Knowing what is important to us can help us be in touch with those things that give us meaning.

8. ART. The challenge of loving music and co-creating it helps us re-experience the joy of this special language.

9. EMOTIONS. Experiencing our feelings toward the many aspects of the music profession can help us stay in touch with the things we love and dislike.

10. FEELING CALM. Relaxing while experiencing the performance of music is a practical goal for auditioners.

11. MERGE INTO THE MUSIC. It is important to be comfortable with your experience of yourself in the act of playing, so that your musical experience can come through.[50]

---

[50]Green, loc. cit., 64.

12. EVERY MOMENT PROVIDES AN OPPORTUNITY TO LEARN AND GROW. Trust the musician in you and recognize opportunities for appropriate change.[51]

13. FIND THE BEAUTY THAT AFFECTS YOU THE MOST. Be in touch with what it is in music that attracts you.

14. KNOW WHO YOU ARE. Being in touch with what you want and need can add great insight to a performance. Actualizing your inspiration is a duty of a performing artist.[52]

15. REVEALING OUR FEARS EXPOSES OUR VULNERABILITY AND GIVES US STRENGTH AT THE SAME TIME. Vulnerability houses deep inside a basic honesty, a naked truth. This truth is strength, as it is the mystery solved, and reality exposed.[53]

The final suggestions shared above, if considered carefully, can help us with every other aspect dealt with in this book. When we have discovered what makes us "tick," we will then be able to make the choices we need to in order to really LIVE rather than just EXIST. More specifically, we can decide which techniques will work for us, as individuals, in fighting audition and performance nervousness.

An attempt has been made in the preceeding chapters to share a composite of methods from many sources to reduce the stress of auditioning. The fact that so many books and articles have been written on the subject demonstrates that stagefright is a problem which many people share. The bibliography in the next few pages shows only a portion of the available materials which have been published on related subjects. A large number of sources were used here so that the reader can follow up and seek further information regarding a particular section of interest.

Before succumbing to the stress of auditioning and performing in public by ceasing to participate, consider reflecting on and experimenting with, the ideas in the above chapters. It is this writer's hope that the suggestions, facts, and thoughts included in this work

---

[51]Ibid. 112.
[52]Triplett, loc. cit., 103-04.
[53]Ibid. . 97

have simply served the purpose of shedding new light for anyone in need.

THE AUTHOR

Dr. Stuart E. Dunkel

Dr. Stuart Dunkel has held the position of principal oboist in the Opera Company of Boston, the Hong Kong Philharmonic, and the Florida Gulf Coast Symphony. He performed and recorded with the Boston Symphony Orchestra from 1974 to 1981 and held the position of solo English Hornist with the Boston Pops Esplanade Orchestra under the direction of Arthur Fiedler and John Williams during those years. After graduating from Boston University in 1975, in addition to playing with the Boston Opera, Dr. Dunkel also performed with the Boston Ballet, the Springfield and Rhode Island Symphonies. During this period he taught at the All-Newton Music School, the South Shore Conservatory, and the Longy School of Music. In 1977 he formed a co-operative ensemble, THE PRO ARTE CHAMBER ORCHESTRA OF BOSTON, which is currently in its 11th season.

After a season with the Hong Kong Philharmonic, he joined the Gulf Coast Symphony in 1983 where he formed a second chamber orchestra, THE TAMPA BAY CHAMBER SOLOISTS, now in its 5th year. Dr. Dunkel received the Master of Music degree from The Mannes College of Music in 1985 and completed the Doctor of Musical Arts degree from the Juilliard School in 1987. While residing in New York he performed with the Metropolitan Opera Orchestra, the New York Philharmonic, the Mostly Mozart Festival, the New Jersey and Westfield Symphonies, The Little Orchestra Society, the Naumberg and Brooklyn Opera Orchestras, and other free-lance groups. Stuart has been soloist with the Detroit Symphony, the Hong Kong Philharmonic, and the Pro Arte Chamber Orchestra.

He received awards and scholarships at the Tanglewood, Blossom, Aspen, and Sarasota Festivals, and at Boston University, Mannes, and Juilliard. His oboe teachers have included Elaine Douvas, John Mack, Harold Gomberg, Ralph Gomberg, Robert Bloom, and Harry Shulman. Upon returning to Boston in 1987, Stuart has performed as acting assistant principal oboist of the Boston Symphony Orchestra and the Boston Pops during the '87-'88 season. He can be seen on many of the "Evening at Pops" television broadcasts. He also resumed his principal oboe position at the Opera Company and joined the faculties of Boston University, The New England and Boston Conservatories of Music and the Longy Music School, where he was chairman of the wind department in 1987.

Among other activities, Stuart is an active composer specializing in solo and chamber works for the oboe. He also paints in oils and has had three shows in New York. Stuart owns the business, "OBOE CANE AND REEDS BY STUART DUNKEL," which supplies oboe products to oboists world-wide.

‹ೞ›

BIBLIOGRAPHY

Aaron, Stephen. Stage Fright. Chicago: The University of Chicago Press, 1986.

American Orchestra League. "A Fair Hearing: Three Views of the Symphony Orchestra Audition." Symphony Magazine: October/November 1983, 10-14.

Anthony, Robert. Total Self-Confidence. San Diego: Berkley Publishing Corporation, 1979.

Bandler, Richard and John Grinder. Frogs into Princes. Utah: Real People Press, 1979.

_____. Using Your Brain. Utah: Real People Press, 1985.

Barker, Sarah. The Alexander Technique. New York: Bantam Books, 1978.

Baxter, Marty. Over-Come Stage Fright. New York: Bradley Publications, 1982.

Branden, Nathaniel. The Psychology of Self-Esteem. New York: Bantam Books, 1981.

Brenner, Elizabeth. Winning by Letting Go. San Diego: Harcourt Brace Jovanovich, 1985.

Brown, B. Stress and the Art of Biofeedback. New York: Harper and Row, 1977.

Burns, David D., M.D. Feeling Good. New York: William Morrow and Co., Inc., 1980.

_____. The New Mood Therapy. New York: The New American Library, Inc., 1980.

Channing L. Bete Co., Inc. About Stress Management. Massachusetts: Channing L. Bete Co., 1986.

_____. What Everyone Should Know About Depression. Massachusetts: Channing L. Bete Co., Inc., 1980.

Colgrass, Michael. "Speaking of Music." Music Magazine. May/June 1981, 38.

_____. "You Should See Yourself." Jam Magazine. December 1981, 12.

_____. "Circle of Excellence." Jam Magazine. 38.

_____. "Coping with Stage Fright". Music Magazine. December 1981, 38.

Davies, J. B. The Psychology of Music. California: Stanford University Press, 1978.

Ellis, Albert. A New Guide to Rational Living. New Jersey: Prentice-Hall, Inc., 1975.

Emery, Stewart. The Owner's Manual For Your Life. New York: Pocket Books, 1982.

Fensterheim, Herbert. Stop Running Scared! New York: Dell Publishing Co., Inc., 1977.

Fosse, B. Audition. New York: Bantam Books, 1980.

Gabbard, Glen. "Stage Fright: Symptoms and Causes." American Organist. March 1983, 11-15.

Galway, Timothy. Sports: The Inner Way to Reducing Stress. Cassette on Cognetics.

Gaylin, Willard. Feelings. New York: Ballantine Books, 1979.

Golan, J. "The Art of Auditioning." The Instrumentalist. May, 1976, 22-27.

Graffman, Naomi. "StageFright." Horizon Magazine. September, 1981, 52-56.

Green, Barry. The Inner Game of Music. New York: Anchor Press, 1986.

Hall, Edward. The Silent Language. New York: Fawcett World Library, 1959.

Harris, Thomas. I'm OK-You're OK. New York: Avon Books, 1969.

Havas, Kato. Stage Fright: Its Causes and Cures. London: Bosworth and Co., 1953.

Hittleman, Richard. Guide to Yoga Meditaion. New York: Bantam Books, 1969.

Hunt, Gordon. How to Audition. New York: Harper and Row, 1977.

Keller, Barbara. "Stage Fright and How to Conquer It." Keynote . 21-25.

Lilly, John. Simulations of God. New York: Simon and Schuster, 1975.

Lorayne, Harry. Secrets of Mind Power. New York: Signet, 1975.

Madow, Leo. Anger. New York: Charles Scribner's Sons, 1972.

Maltz, Maxwell. Psycho-Cybernetics. New York: Prentice-Hall, Inc., 1960.

Markus, Tom. The Professional Actor. New York: Drama Book Specialists, 1979.

Matson, Katinka. The Working Actor. New York: Penguin Books, 1984.

May, Rollo. Man's Search for Himself. New York: Delta Books, 1973.

McCamy, John. Human Life Styling. New York: Harper and Row, 1975.

McKay, Matthew. Thoughts and Feelings. California: New Harbinger Publications, 1981.

Morris, Eric. Being and Doing. California: Spelling Publications, 1981.

Nelson, Jane. Understanding. California: Sunrise Press, 1986.

Parker, Rolland. Emotional Common Sense. New York: Harper and Row, 1981.

Pietsch, William. Human Be-ing. New York: Signet Books, 1975.

Rhinehart, Luke. The Book of EST. New York: Holt, Rinehart and Winston, 1976.

Ried, Wendy. Auditions Are Just the Beginning: A Career Guide to the Orchestra. Association of Canadian Orchestras: Toronto, Ontario, 1981.

Ristad, Eloise. A Soprano on Her Head. Utah: Real People Press, 1982.

Rodale Press, ed. Twentyone Surefire Stress Releasers. Pennsylvania: Rodale Press, 1983.

Rubin, Theodore. The Anger Book. New York: Macmillan Publishing Co., 1969.

Sarnoff, Dorothy. Make the Most of Your Best. New York: Doubleday and Company, 1981.

Satir, Virginia. Your Many Faces. California: Celestial Arts, 1978.

Segal, Jeanne. Living Beyond Fear. California: Newcastle Publishing Co., 1984.

Shurtleff, Michael. Audition. New York: Bantam Books, 1978.

Siegleman, Ellen. Personal Risk. New York: Harper and Row, 1983.

Silver, Fred. Auditioning for the Musical Theatre. New York: Newmarket Press, 1985.

Steptoe, Andrew. "Performance Anxiety." The Musical Times. August 1982. 537-541.

Triplett, Robert. Stage-fright: Letting It Work for You. Chicago: Nelson-Hall, 1983.

Tubesing, Donald. Kicking Your Stress Habits. Minnesota: Bolger Publications, 1981.

Tuck, Marilyn. "Stress Management and Musical Performance." The American Organist. March, 1983, 54-56.

Tutko, Thomas. Sports Psyching. Los Angeles: J.P. Tarcher, Inc., 1976.

Vairo, Linda. Stamp Out Stress. New York: Manor Books, 1978.

Viscott, David. Risking. New York: Simon and Schuster, 1977.

_____. The Language of Feelings. New York: Pocket Books, 1976.

Walster, Elaine. A New Look at Love. Massachusetts: Addison-Wesley Publishing Company, 1978.

Weekes, Claire. Peace From Nervous Suffering. New York: Hawthorn Books, 1983.

Wilson, R. Reid. Don't Panic. New York: Harper and Row, 1986.

Zane, Manual. Your Phobia. Washington, D.C.: American Psychiatric Press, 1984.

Zimbardo, Philip. Shyness. New York: Jove Books, 1977.

Zlotkin, Frances. "Stage Fright and the Performing Musician." New York, 1985.